A Child Called Wendy

SHAUN ALLAN

ISBN: 978-1-910484-21-0

DEDICATION

For my brother, whom I probably resented a little as a child (*I had to push him around in his pram when he was a baby and I was eight years old*), but I love as an adult. And, when we're together, childish humour and antics have been known to ensue.

CONTENTS

"When childhood dies, its corpses are adults."

Brian Aldiss

1 NOW

They were unmoving. Their eyes stared forwards, ignoring her question. They didn't care. They never would, not anymore.

Still, she repeated herself. She insisted on manners when people dealt with her and offered the same consideration back.

"Would you like sugar or sweetener?" she asked. "Or are you sweet enough?"

The last comment made her chuckle. It always had, even when it had been her father asking her, as he often did before his untimely death.

They still didn't answer or look at her. She waited for a few more seconds, then put the small China bowl (only the best for her guests) down.

"That's fine," she said, keeping her impatience to herself. "I'll let you do it. Don't let it get cold."

They would, though. It would cool to the point it formed a thin skin that clung to the insides of the cup, doing its best to leave a stained ring. It wouldn't work. Wendy was ever vigilant for such things and was scrupulous in her washing both cutlery and crockery. A stain or dried on crumb of food would never pass her inspection however hard they tried to hide themselves.

She left them to it. Let them sulk and pout. They'd get over it. She'd nuke their drinks in the microwave later if they still wanted them. It was a practice that seemed like sacrilege to her. Tea was meant to be drunk at the time it was made, not reheated in a metal box that poured radiation over its contents. But, she was not one to waste anything. And if they were going to behave like children, then they didn't deserve to be treated like adults. Their punishment would be the irradiated liquid, heated to a temperature that would cause taste buds to blister in fright.

Closing the door, Wendy sighed. Why did they have to be so difficult? She was doing her best to please them. She'd bought their favourite cakes and biscuits. She was using her very special crockery, even the set she'd bought when she moved into her first house with her then husband. It was one of the most expensive tea sets in the store and she had taken great care with it ever since. She still had the box it came in and even the receipt. To her eyes, tired though they often were, the colours were still just as vibrant.

They should be grateful.

Wendy shrugged. It was their loss. She was, as her husband, Arthur, would say, *'the hostess with the mostess'*, so they must be sulking. If that were the case, she'd wait it out. Her patience had grown thin over the years since he'd died. Thin enough to peek through if it were raised to her face. She would, once upon a time, have smiled at Arthur's oft repeated joke. She'd have giggled when he followed it with a light smack to her bum. Both things bored her, but Arthur didn't suspect it. She loved him dearly and made sure he never would.

It was time to clean house, something Wendy was fastidious about, at least as long as her hip would let her. There was minimal dust, but she liked each room to be spotless in case she had visitors. She loved visitors, and her tea and scones were legendary.

As the vacuum cleaner thrummed whilst sucking up the odd crumb or fallen hair, she sang to herself. It was an old song, one whose lyrics had changed slightly over the years with each retelling. Wendy's mother had sung it to her and, so the story went, *her* mother sang it to *her* and so on for around six generations. It was simple, with only a couple of verses and a chorus shimmied in, and had never been either played on the radio or streamed to a smartphone. As far as she knew, it had yet to be put down in any physical form whatsoever. It had been made up by Gran'pa Sophiss over a hundred and fifty years before and Wendy loved the song.

The vacuuming took only a few minutes to finish, and then Wendy was onto the dusting. Armed with her trusty can of spray polish and yellow cloth, she set her sights on the shelves of her bookcase.

Wendy's eyes weren't as good as they had been once upon a time. Reading gave her a headache after only a few pages. She had tried audiobooks, but found they just sent her to sleep, and she was forever having to rewind to find the last part she could remember. Luckily, television sets had grown in size, with their prices not changing at the same speed. It meant she was still able to watch her few favourite programs but, even then, she was prone to needing paracetamol after any real length of viewing.

The dusting took less time than the vacuuming and the supplies were back in the cupboard under the sink in time for the kettle she'd switched on to click off, ready. As she was already putting some old clothes - or old*est* clothes, given she didn't often buy her anything new to wear, so all her clothes were *old* – in a bag for a nearby charity shop, she continued with that. The water in the kettle would remain hot for a little while. It may even have cooled enough for her to drink her tea immediately.

She checked the collection date on the charity bag. Wednesday, two days hence. She'd put them out tomorrow night, in case she forgot on the actual day, but not before. She didn't trust them to still be there. People would steal anything if they had the chance, even the tired clothes of an old woman.

She poked her head into the dining room.

"Last chance for that cup of tea. Don't be shy, now." A pause to give them a chance to respond. "I'm having one myself anyway, so it's no bother."

There was still no response. Wendy hated rude people and wondered why she'd allowed them to enter her home. She was too nice. Too easy going. She always had been and had thought about being more assertive, but she was too old to change her ways. She liked being nice. She enjoyed conversation and meeting people. A 'people person'. That's what she was. She couldn't remember where she'd heard that phrase or who'd used it in relation to her, but it was true. She liked people.

Of course, it hadn't always been that way. As she stirred her tea, taking the used bag out and depositing it in the kitchen bin, she thought back. She did that more and more in recent years. Her advancing years weighed heavily on her stooping shoulders and she liked to let her mind wander back to a time where she wasn't so... weathered. When storms hadn't battered her shores and eroded her landscapes.

Back to before the first death.

Wendy had been young, then. In the nine years of her life, she'd seen her father exactly seventeen times. Four of those had been her birthdays, numbers 3, 4, 6 and 8. Though she was still young, she knew the chances of seeing him any more after that were slim. Usually, her parent's arguments only lasted for a short period of time before one or the other would walk out, the issues behind the harsh words would fester until the next call or text or visit, but would never be settled.

For her eighth birthday, her father had bought her a puppy, completely against the wishes of his ex wife. *Muppet* had been Wendy's best friend for one year and, coincidentally, seventeen days. George, Wendy's father, had never physically hurt either mother or daughter, but words could cut deeper than any knife. The young girl had been on the receiving end of vicious rants that had left her crying for several nights. They'd left her mother, Carol, crying and bruised.

She, Wendy, was sure she wasn't the useless, stupid girl Eddie, George's replacement, would tell her she was. She wasn't ugly or fat. Boys *would* be interested in her when she grew up. And so what if she ended up like her mother? To the nine year old – or four or six or eight – Carol was a soldier in a war she could never win. Yet one she kept fighting.

She was thinking about one of those fights when the knock on the front door made her realise she was still stirring her cup. She smiled to herself.

"Silly old fool."

Dropping the teaspoon in the sink, she went to see who was interrupting her cuppa, casting a brief glance at the dining room door to ensure it was closed fully. They didn't like to be disturbed.

"Hello officer," she said to the young policeman whose fist was raised to knock again.

2 THEN

To a six year old, a police officer is intimidating. They're like the Child Catcher from Chitty Chitty Bang Bang. They can drag you away and lock you up if they hear you swearing or see you stealing or catch you out of school during school hours.

The one who was standing at the door when the young Wendy answered it instantly made her nervous. She had to think through her actions of that day and the one before. She'd been at school when she was meant to. She would never steal anything and she had yet to pluck up the courage to use a 'naughty word'. She felt guilty even though she was certain she'd done nothing she shouldn't do.

"Is your father in, young lady?" the officer said.

Wendy liked being called a 'young lady'. It made her feel grown up. As such, she smiled when she nodded.

"He's in the bathroom," she said.

"Wendy!"

"Shit!"

The words were exclaimed simultaneously, the former by her mother and the latter by her father. Wendy had to think who she was more scared of, the police or her parents. It was close, but the officer won. Her mother and father could punish her, but the policeman could put her in prison and flush the key down the toilet. It had happened to Donnie Bleakson's big brother. He was never going to get out of prison, and all the things they said about him, the armed robbery and the car theft, were lies. It just showed, you didn't mess with the police.

"May I come in, m'dear?" the policeman said, smiling warmly.

Wendy didn't get the chance to reply. Her mother crashed through the doorway to the living room and pushed in front of the little girl.

"He's not here," she said sharply.

"Your daughter said he was. Can I come in and speak to him?"

"I said, he's not here. She's mistaken."

"But, Mummy…" Wendy began. She was cut off by a rough push, sending her reeling through the door her mother had just come through.

"She's mistaken," Wendy's mother repeated.

Her name was Carol, but she would change it depending on which man she was with at the time. She didn't want them to know who she really was. They might find her that way, and ask for their wallets or watches or phones back.

"Mrs. Whipnale, I heard his voice. Please let me in. I just want a word."

The officer took a step forward, but the woman stood firm, blocking him.

"I said, she's mistaken and he's not here. So fuck off and pick on some real criminals, instead of making stories up about my Eddie."

The officer stood without saying anything. He could tell her that the stories were not made up and she knew it. He could say that she needed to stop defending such a lowlife and concentrate on bringing up her children and treating them better. And to not let the two come into contact with each other if she actually gave a shit about the little ones.

"OK, Mrs. Whipnale. I'll leave you to it. Have a good day."

"It will be now you're fucking off."

The front door was slammed and so was the one to the living room as Carol stormed through it.

Fucking police. Victimisation, that's what it was. Eddie was just trying to make enough money to look after them all. Benefits would only go so far. They didn't drink much, and only bought knock off cigs from their friends. And they only stole from the big stores. The ones with insurance. The ones who counted breakages and thefts in their figures. They wouldn't miss them, and if they did, fuck 'em. They charged too much anyways.

Slowly, Wendy opened the door. She wasn't shaking. She didn't do that anymore, and her bladder was empty, as she'd only been to the toilet a few minutes before. She wouldn't wet herself. The fear was still there. The knowledge. It still hurt as much, but she was better at not showing it. She felt she was trembling inside, but the shakes weren't making through her skin to the outside.

Her mother was sitting on the large sofa. A kick-back, she called it. It was deep enough for her to be able to sit on it and tuck her legs under comfortably. She would rest her mug of tea on the side of her bent knee, an area that could take any heat a boiled kettle could throw at it. She'd watch the stream of talk shows, house makeovers and tabloid TV, only moving to urinate or fill up her cup.

A cup that was empty.

She didn't turn. She just held up her hand, with the mug sitting on the palm. Wendy knew the signal and was relieved. There'd be no reprisals for speaking to or even opening the door to the *pig*. She took the cup gingerly, holding her breath, and stepped back.

"Why did you do that, Wendy?"

Her step father had come out from the bathroom, now the coast was clear. The usual cigarette hung from his lower lip, sticking there as if surgically attached. As she watched, the ash detached itself from the end and dropped to the floor. Her father followed her line of sight and used the toe of his shoe to rub the ash into the carpet. His arms were folded, and he was leaning against the door frame. He returned his attention to her.

Wendy's retreat had stopped when she heard him speak. His question was spoken evenly. Calmly. Thus, it terrified her. The man lost his temper many times. He would beat his wife while telling her, alternately, that she deserved it and he was sorry. She didn't mind. He was a good father and he loved her. Wendy saw it all, but she wasn't fooled into believing, as her mother had told her on multiple occasions, that it was a part of life. Relationships were like that. Love was shown in a variety of ways (or 'shit loads', to quote Carol's phrase). If you got a black eye, you learned how to use makeup to disguise it.

No, Wendy wasn't fooled. She saw her mother cry. She saw the bruises through the gap in the door. And Carol wasn't as adept at makeup as she let herself think.

She thought her parents did love her. They maybe didn't know how to show it. Or care to.

"I assume you're going to answer me, girl?"

Wendy jumped. She fumbled to not drop her mother's cup, and was lucky enough to catch it before it fell. She saw Eddie smile. She didn't like his smile.

"Sorry daddy."

"I know you are, baby girl. So, why did you do that?"

That' could be any number of things. She always seemed to be doing something to disappoint or anger him. In this case, however, *that* was obvious.

"I didn't know it was going to be a policeman when I opened the door, daddy."

"That's why you let us do it, instead. But you know that, don't you?"

Wendy nodded., She did know it. She was always supposed to let her parents answer the door to any callers. They didn't want any surprises.

"So why didn't you?"

"Because I wanted to be a big girl and help you."

"That's nice of you. Isn't that nice of her darl'?" Carol nodded without looking away from the television. "Look at me when I'm talking to you, bitch!" It was Carol's turn to jump.

"Yes, baby. It's very nice!"

Eddie held Carol's gaze before looking back at the girl he'd graciously taken on as his daughter, dismissing his wife.

"It's very nice. Still, the police like to make stories up about mummy and daddy, so they're not your friends, are they?"

"No daddy. They're not our friends."

"So, you won't do it again, will you?"

A shake of the girl's head.

"Excellent. That's my girl. Now, why don't you make mummy a cuppa."

"Are you sure, daddy?"

"I'm sure. Go on."

Wendy didn't run, but her haste was barely contained. She was in the kitchen before either of her parents could change their minds and give out the punishment.

The kettle was always filled. The rule was, you always had to top the water level up once you'd used it. It had to be ready to go when a new drink was needed. Wendy pressed the button to switch it on. She pulled over a chair to stand on, lifting it rather than scraping the floor, and used it to be able to access the tea bags and sugar.

Once the tea was made, Wendy carefully took it through to her mother. Carol took it impatiently, still smarting from the harsh words of her husband. She'd pay for them later. It was all the brat's fault.

"Let me look at that," said Eddie.

He'd returned to the bathroom and was in the process of shaving. Half of his face was covered in shaving cream and the other half was smooth and hairless. Carol held the mug out for inspection.

"I think that's a bit too milky, don't you baby?"

Carol looked at the liquid. It looked fine to her, but she wasn't going to disagree.

"It is a bit," she answered.

"I think Wendy would like something else to wear, don't you?"

Carol frowned, just as Wendy did. What had clothes to do with the amount of milk in a cup of tea? Eddie could see the confusion so decided to elaborate. He walked over to his wife, bringing his hand out sharply. The woman flinched, shrinking backwards. The hand didn't make contact with the face, though. Instead, smiling broadly, he took the mug.

He turned to his daughter, drew his hand back and brought it forward sharply. The hot liquid hit Wendy full in the face before dripping down to soak her clothes. Wendy screamed, her face rapidly flushing red from the heat. She brought her hands up to wipe her face, desperately wanting to run to the bathroom so she could bathe her cheeks and brow, hoping she hadn't been burned.

She daren't move. If she tried to run, her father would grab her arm and punish her. She had to stay put. Her face was stinging and she could feel the warmth of the drenched material, but it was secondary to the pain her father could cause.

Wendy looked at her mother, wishing that, for once, she'd stand up for her daughter. Carol looked shocked, but said nothing. If anything, she was lamenting the waste of a good cuppa.

"Look what you've done, Wendy," Eddie said, pointing. "Ruined your uniform."

"S… Sorry daddy. I'll go get changed."

"And cause even more washing for your mother? I don't think so. Besides, you'll be late."

"But..."

Wendy regretted the start of the sentence as soon as the word had left her mouth. She'd managed to stop herself from saying anything else, but the word was out there now. Lost to her. Evidence that she was about to argue with her father.

"Get off to school, now dear," Eddie said quietly.

Again, Wendy looked to her mother for support, but Carol was staring at the tea stain on the carpet. The girl wished she could go into her bedroom and come out to find her parents had been replaced by strangers. Even if she didn't know them, it would be better than reality. Her hesitation was picked up by Eddie.

"Now, dear," he repeated through gritted teeth.

Wendy nodded, picked up her school bag, kissed both her parents on their cheeks and left.

Maybe school would be better.

3 NOW

"Good afternoon," said the police officer. He smiled, but his face didn't reflect the gesture. It remained serious and it was this that Wendy responded to.

"Can I help you?"

"We're looking for a missing person. We're doing house to house enquiries in case anyone has seen him."

"I'm afraid I don't get many visitors, officer. And I don't get out much."

"Of course, madam. But perhaps you've noticed him? He's tall, slim build and has a small crescent scar over his right eye."

"I don't recall seeing anyone of that description."

"Well, one of your neighbours seems to think they saw someone of that description come to your house a few days ago."

Wendy frowned and scratched the side of her head. She looked confused.

"Did they? Which day would that be?"

"They were unsure. Wednesday or Thursday, perhaps?"

"Well, on Wednesday, I always go into town to do my weekly shop. I'm out most of the afternoon. Oh, and I had my hair done. Do you like it?"

"It's very nice, madam. Now, what about Thursday?"

"Now you mention it, I believe I did have a visitor. My old memory keeps playing hide and seek with me nowadays, you know."

The policeman smiled. She reminded him of his grandmother. He would always have to give his opinion on her hair and he could imagine this woman having some fresh baked delicacies in her oven that he was keeping her from.

"You did? Can you tell me anything about him?"

"He was a lovely young man," Wendy said, nodding. "He was very polite and quite pleasant."

"Can you tell me what he wanted?"

"He'd stood in something unmentionable in the park. Some people just shouldn't have dogs if they're not going to pick up after them. Makes you wonder what their own houses are like."

"Indeed not, madam. It's a real nuisance."

"Absolutely. He asked if I had anything he could use to clean his shoe, so I gave him some water, a cloth and brush."

"He was wearing shoes? What else was he wearing."

"Well, I say shoe, but it was one of those training shoes the young ones like to wear. White with a blue scribble on the side."

The officer smiled again. He always found memory fascinating. A person could be adamant they didn't remember any details of a situation yet, once you had enticed them to talk about it, it was surprising just how much they actually did remember.

"Was there anything else?"

"He just wore jeans and a dark blue jumper. I thought he was terribly underdressed for the weather. These young ones think they're better than dear old Mother Nature, don't they?"

"Indeed, madam."

"I offered him a cup of tea and a biscuit. I thought he needed warming up and a few calories on his figure wouldn't go amiss."

"Oh, so he came in?"

"Oh no," Wendy said. "He refused. He said he was on his way to the pub to meet some friends. He did thank me, though, which I thought was nice."

"Did he say which pub?"

"Well, I'm afraid he didn't, but if he was on foot, it would likely be the Wheatsheaf, wouldn't it?"

The Wheatsheaf was situated at the end of the long road Wendy's house and the park opposite led off. It was at a busy junction and had once been the place to go if you were a student at the nearby college. It had since been given a makeover in decoration and menu in a bid to entice a more mature customer. The attempt had worked and it was now renowned for its atmosphere and food.

"Quite possibly," the officer said, nodding thoughtfully.

"Is that all, Officer? My bladder is reminding me it needs to be emptied."

"No, that'll be all, madam. If anything else comes to mind, please give me a call, would you?"

He handed the woman a card, which she took and read.

"Of course I will, Officer Patel."

"Call me Ravendra, please."

"Ravendra. You can call me Mrs. Somerset."

The policeman couldn't help but grin at her enforced formality given as if being quite the opposite. He managed to hide his mouth with his hand before she could see it.

"Thank you, Mrs. Somerset. Have a good day."

Wendy nodded and, after he'd turned to leave, closed the door. She moved to the room her guests were in and entered. She stood in front of one. A man wearing jeans, a dark jumper and white trainers. The scribble on the side was, in fact, red, which Wendy knew quite well. It wouldn't do to give too many details away. It might look suspicious.

"A nice policeman was just here for you, dear," she said gently. "Don't worry, though. He's gone now."

She turned and picked up the paint brush laying on the sheet of newspaper on the coffee table. Dipping it in the tin of varnish next to it, she returned her attention to her guest.

"Let's just give you that other coat I promised. We want you looking your best, don't we?"

She held the brush up and began to carefully apply the varnish to his face, neck and hands. She used a cloth to wipe away any excess that might want to drip off either onto the floor or onto his clothes. Once she was finished, she set the brush back down.

"There you go. It won't be long before you're all done, then you'll be just like the others. Shiny, bright and just perfect!"

Wendy looked around the room at those others, smiling broadly. It was such a lovely tea party. She really did enjoy entertaining visitors, and did her very best to be the hostess with the mostest.

"I'll put the kettle on, lovelies. If you think it will suit me, that is."

She giggled, a high tinkle of sound that would have made the policeman wonder just how old she really was. The laugh sounded far too young to have come from the aged throat of the woman.

"I'll be right back," Wendy said. "And I've got a treat for you all. Custard creams!"

She left the room and went to the kitchen. She emptied the water from the kettle, always boiling from fresh, refilled it and switched it on. The packet of custard cream biscuits had only been opened the day before, so she didn't mind using them. Any more than three days, and they'd have to be new too. Soft biscuits, unless they were cookies, and reboiled water were definite no goes for her. She had standards and didn't want to disappoint her guests by giving them anything that might resemble second best.

Of course, Wendy used her best cups. She used to enjoy tea in China cups, which she'd drink as hot as she could stand it and, if the drink had cooled before it could be finished, she'd nuke it in the microwave to boost its temperature. She relaxed the actual cup itself to change best to good. A mug sacrificed elegance for volume and it was a sacrifice she was willing to make. That was, until she was in the company of others. Then the China was brought out, given a thorough wash, before being used to serve Wendy's speciality.

Tea.

Except, not just tea. This was tea with a special ingredient. Her own recipe.

The 'Somerset Specialitea', she liked to call it. She'd laugh, but she'd be the only one. Her guests rarely, she discovered, found it funny.

Once the drinks were made, and a small plate was filled with the biscuits, Wendy took them through. It was always dark in the sitting room. The curtains, just like those all over the house, were thick and lined. It kept the utility bills down and ensured she was never cold. It also meant she didn't need to put the radiators on. That would have been unfortunate.

"Here we are," she said, brightly. "I told you I'd treat you., Don't eat them all at once, you'll give yourself indigestion. We wouldn't want that, now would we?"

None of her guests answered. None looked at her or even responded to her comment. Not a single one would take so much as a sip from the tea she offered, or consume a single crumb from the custard creams.

How could they?

4 THEN

School *was* better, and only a couple of children commented on her clothes before her form tutor took her to one side and gave her a clean shirt from Lost Property. She would make sure she changed back before going home.

Going to school was meant to be some of the best years of one's life. If you asked many pupils, they'd say it was the worst time possible. They'd hate it. The rules. The work. The teachers and bullying and peer pressure. Once they left and had to face the 'real world', with responsibilities, work, bills and so on, they realise how simple their youth actually was.

For the young girl, her viewpoint differed to many of her fellow pupils. She *loved* school. She would happily bury herself in lessons and there wasn't a single teacher she had an issue with. Although she was occasionally reprimanded for speaking or daydreaming, Wendy didn't mind. She welcomed it, in fact.

It meant someone was paying attention to her.

She had few friends. Friends wanted to have sleepovers. Friends wanted to call for you to see if you were coming out to play. Wendy didn't want to expose anyone else to her parents. The visiting child would be safe from drinks being thrown at them or derisory comments and, possibly, so would Wendy herself, but there would still be the edge of an atmosphere. She'd be agitated. She'd be waiting. The longer she had to wait, the worse it would be when it came.

Wendy distanced herself from other children and, in turn, they did the same to her. She was strange. She smelled. Her clothes wore stains in the place of colours or patterns. The teachers felt for her, but they seemed to think similarly to the pupils. Wendy was an odd one. Quiet. An outsider. She didn't look after herself. The girl's parents said she always had clean clothes and a full stomach, so why was she dirty and hungry so often? Who knew what she got up to when she was out and about? And, as for the girl walking to school, whatever the weather, her parents had tried to take her, but she had thrown tantrums, screaming and punching until they allowed her to walk alone to school. They didn't like the idea of their poor baby crossing busy roads or walking in the dark, but she refused to be accompanied.

The bite on her mother's arm showed how violent she could be.

No one noticed or commented on the fact the imprint seemed a little large for such a young child.

Wendy, as she would always do, ran most of the way home. She would sprint the full distance if she were able to, but she wasn't the most athletic child, so her lungs and legs couldn't keep up with the demand she wanted to place on them. Her parents knew what time school finished. They knew how long it should take for her to get home, and they wouldn't argue the point. If their friend Terry's son Adam could get home by a certain time, then she should be able to also. So what if he lived within spitting distance of the school grounds? Don't argue girl. Just do it!

So, she ran. She was never fast enough, particularly if the weather was inclement, but did her best. On this day, the rain held off, remaining just a threatening presence above her to spur her on. When she arrived home, she paused just enough for her breath to catch up and slow her panting, or else she'd 'sound like a dog in heat'.

"You in season, girl? You looking for a hound to bag you?"

Wendy had no idea what 'in season' or 'in heat' might mean, but it didn't sound like anything she'd like to be. And she didn't like being compared to a dog. At thirteen, she could run faster as time had passed, but it would never be quick enough.

After a deep, steadying breath, she let herself in. She always tread carefully when she first entered her home, stepping as quietly as she could. She hoped it would give her some time to psyche herself up to facing her parents. Invariably, they would have already heard her coming in, so any element of surprise or chance to avoid detection was already gone. On this occasion, no one called out or swung open the living room door and jumped out at her. She removed her coat and shoes, and hung up her school bag after emptying the remains of her packed lunch in the kitchen bin.

She entered the lounge with the familiar sinking sensation in her belly, as if her heart was falling and had, at that moment, reached her stomach before continuing its descent into the ground. She had imagined there was a grave beneath her, and her heart was sealed in a coffin, still beating. A grave and coffin that moved as she did, so it was always beneath her. Not so she could dig it up and put it back where it should be. No, it was there as a reminder that she'd, once, had a heart that had felt and meant something.

Wendy didn't know if your heart could do that. She'd learned the parts of the body at school, and she knew a heart could break, which sounded painful, but she didn't know if you could keep it in a box – or coffin – and have it still beating. She didn't know, if you put it back, whether or not it would still work.

Her father was asleep on the sofa. He liked to sprawl, moving from his favourite spot on the right hand side to swinging his feet up and taking up all the available space. Wendy's mother always sat in the swivel chair when he did this. She'd bring her feet up, tucking them under her and, by a shake of some kind that Wendy had yet to perfect, swing slowly left and right as she watched the television.

Her mother wasn't asleep and was watching a quiz show. She rarely knew the answers, but thought watching them might make her smarter. Then she'd go on one, win all the money and run away to Barbados. Or maybe Mablethorpe. She liked Mablethorpe. Fish and chips, whipped ice cream with a flake and donkey rides. It was one of the few things she shared with her daughter.

"Hi Mummy," Wendy said, brightly.

Her mother didn't look away from the screen, but mumbled a response. Wendy couldn't make out the words, but didn't mind. She'd been noticed, and that was good enough. On the coffee table were two dinner plates, with smeared ketchup and crumbs coating each. A half empty mug, no longer steaming, stood next to a fully empty glass.

Wendy's heart sank. They'd already eaten. It wasn't the first time this had happened, and she was used to finding something to eat herself, but she was particularly hungry so had hoped to be able to eat with her parents. She turned to go into the kitchen and glanced at her mother.

Carol was looking back at her and had seen the expression of disappointment on her daughter's face. Wendy smiled, attempting to appear as though nothing was wrong. The scowl told her it didn't work.

"What's up with your face?"

"Nothing Mummy. I've just come home."

"I saw you staring at our plates. Being a greedy little shit, as usual?"

"No, Mummy," the girl said. "I was only looking, I promise."

"Don't promise me, when you're clearly lying."

"I'm not! I really was just looking." Wendy kept her voice steady, holding back the wave of emotion and fear that was building inside of her small frame.

"You were staring and wondering where yours was. I'm not bloody blind. And don't you dare use that tone with me, young lady."

Wendy thought about protesting, but knew her mother would only see it as arguing, something she wouldn't tolerate from her daughter. The word of both parents was law, and Wendy knew better than to go against it. Even when she'd done or said nothing wrong, she took the reprimand. To do otherwise would only make things worse.

"Kitchen table," Carol snapped.

Wendy frowned, not knowing what the random phrase could mean. Her mother slammed her palm down on the arm of the sofa and leaned forward fiercely. The girl took a step back.

"Your tea is on the kitchen table. Go get it and stop complaining."

"I'm not…"

"Not hungry? Not complaining? Don't finish that sentence, 'cos you'll still be lying, and you can sod off to bed without anything."

Wendy nodded and did her best to smile again.

"Thank you, Mummy," she said.

Carol had already turned back to the television, her daughter dismissed.

5 THEN

Wendy's meal was cold, the not properly drained grease the chips had been cooked in congealing. A half dozen garden peas accompanied the three cheap and not very cheerful fish fingers. Usually, this would have been one of her favourite meals but, with there not being enough heat remaining to cause the faintest mist of steam, every bite seemed to stick in her throat.

"Wendy!"

A sharp smack against the back of her head woke her and she lifted her head from her plate. The remains of a half eaten fish finger fell from her cheek onto her lap. She blinked, not sure what had happened, picked it up and started to eat it.

"Don't be disgusting!" snapped Eddie, slapping it from her hand and onto the floor. "Now, pick it up!"

Wendy, trying to hold the tears back from the stinging of her hand and the throbbing in the back of her head, picked up the food and put it slowly on her plate. She wasn't sure whether she should eat it or leave it, so waited for further instructions. Before her father could give her any, Carol stormed through.

"What's she bloody done now?"

"Fell asleep with her head in her food. Can you believe it?"

"So that's what she thinks of the effort I put into cooking for her? Too boring to eat, eh?"

"No, Mummy. Of course not."

"Of course not? You calling me a liar? Look at the state of you. Food on your face, tea stains on your shirt and peas and salt in your damn hair!"

"You disgust me," Eddie said, sneering. "How did we end up with a kid like you?"

"Tell me about it, baby," Carol nodded, her hands on her hips.

"Get yourself to bed, before I lose my temper with you," Eddie ordered.

Wendy stood slowly, not wanting to ask either of her parents to move, but unable to get past.

"Can I have a bath, please?"

"No, you can't. You can wear your tea to bed, like you deserve. It'll give you a snack if you get hungry, though I don't know why I'm being so generous."

The girl looked at her mother and smiled.

"Thank you Mummy."

It was the right thing to say. Anything else would have been seen as being 'too big for her boots', something she often, it appeared, seemed to be. Her mother stepped aside, allowing her through.

"Move it, or I'll change my mind."

Wendy scurried out of the kitchen and was in her bedroom with the door closed before she let the held breath out. She changed out of her clothes, pleased to have clean ones in her chest of drawers. Though her parents had refused permission to clean herself, she risked wiping her hands and face with baby wipes. They wouldn't remember in the morning, in all likelihood, so she felt fairly safe in doing so. She was looking forward to the next day. Swimming lessons took place in the morning and, though she wasn't the strongest swimmer, she was fairly adept. She loved the freedom being in the water gave her. She had no idea if mermaids existed, but she could pretend she was one.

The next morning, Wendy was up and dressed and had prepared her parents' drinks ready for them coming out of their rooms. She wanted to give neither of them any reason to pick fault with her. The swimming lesson was something to look forward to and she wanted a bright, reprimand free morning beforehand. Carol and Eddie didn't notice she had clean clothes on, and Wendy had made sure exactly the right amount of milk and sugar was in their brews. She'd made and eaten her breakfast, and washed, dried and put away the pots. Her parents didn't comment on any of this, but at least they didn't see or look for any issues. She left with a smile from her and grunts from them.

The school provided a coach to the swimming pool. It had plenty of room for the pupils to sit together with their friends and talk or laugh noisily for the entire journey each way. It also had the space for Wendy to get on last and find a seat by herself. Occasionally, she'd find someone beside her. Occasionally, they'd be nice – Wendy wasn't the only one who saw herself as an outcast – but sometimes, they'd feign pleasantries in order to tease or humiliate her in one form or another. This morning, the seat next to her remained empty. It was apparently too early or the sun was too bright to waste time picking on one of the year's most obvious targets. She was even able to get herself changed without anyone making fun of her body and its decision to develop a little faster than many of the other girls in her year.

"Julia, Thomas, Petra, Pagan, Isaac and Wendy. Up you go."

They were being taught how to dive properly from height. The lower diving boards, a springboard and one at three metres, had been mastered, but they were easy according to the instructor. If they wanted to really say they could dive, they had to try, and conquer, the five metre monster. For the school children, such a height was intimidating. Simply climbing the steps up to it had more than one freezing and deciding there was no way they could reach the top, let alone leap off into the abyss.

Wendy was nervous. She knew this day would come and had done what she could to prepare herself. Isaac was the school daredevil and nothing seems to faze him, but the others in the group felt the same as Wendy, though they'd not admit it.

"Don't look down," was all the advice the instructor could give.

Wendy wasn't planning on looking anywhere other than the steps right in front of her. She would have to at some point, however. She had to jump off, the prelude to diving. If they could take the leap, they could work up to the next stage. A dive, as graceful and effortless as a champion.

Or as lumpish and *un*graceful as a stone thrown off a bridge into a swamp, as the instructor liked to put it. The comment would garner a collection of nervous laughs from the pupils, with each one imagining that would describe their dismount.

Wendy was fourth in line when they milled around at the back of the large board area. There was a space for a few people to gather while each took their turn to move to the edge and jump, dive or fall off. It was in this space the classmates pushed and shoved to choose their place.

Isaac had gone first, taking the leap with little pause and good form, slipping into the water easily. Thomas went next, though he would happily have waited until last. He couldn't let his friend be the only brave one. His descent wasn't as well made as Isaac's, but it was acceptable. Julia was next. She was the first to really struggle with the jump off. Julia hated heights and always had done. Even when she and her sister had bunk beds, before their family had moved into a house where they could have a room each, Julia had *had* to take the bottom bed.

The others cheered her on, however, with words of encouragement. She smiled, waved, and jumped, with a resounding cheer following her down.

Wendy walked slowly to the edge of the board and looked down. Julia had resurfaced and, once she'd climbed out and was heading back to the steps, she gave Wendy a thumbs up sign. Wendy's smile was half hearted, but she was still thankful for the gesture. If Julia could do it, surely Wendy could too.

She looked back towards her fellow pupils, but they weren't giving her the same send off Julia had. They watched her and she saw Pagan whisper something to Thomas. The boy looked at the whisperer questioningly, then Pagan kissed him lightly on the cheek, a quick peck that made the boy beam and straighten up. He nodded, but didn't say or do anything else. Wendy shrugged inwardly and turned her attention back to the matter at hand – putting herself in the charge of gravity.

She took a deep breath and raised her arms, closing her eyes.

She felt the hands on her costume before realising what was happening. She heard the laughs, from the whole pool, before her mind could process and she could think to open her eyes. She felt the push and heard the shout of anger from the instructor, and then her eyes opened.

The fall seemed to take an age, yet be over in an instant. She had time to cover her exposed breasts but not enough to manoeuvre herself so she would slip into the water as Isaac had done. Instead, she hit the water with force. Smiles turned to looks of horror at her scream as her spectators realised what they'd done. They all heard the sound of her arm breaking, even above the noise of the impact.

The lifeguard closest to her dove in and brought her to the surface, pulling her costume properly back into place. Another joined him and they carefully lifted the injured girl out of the pool before trying to keep the growing crowd back.

Thomas and Pagan were standing next to each other, still up on the 'top board', holding hands.

"Looks like Wendy's not bendy," Pagan said, mostly to herself.

Thomas didn't look away from Wendy, but released his new girlfriend's hand.

6 NOW

Injuries can take a long time to heal. Many leave scars both on the outside and the inside. With some, the scars are purely on the inside. They're not all hidden, though. They rise to the surface in haunted eyes. In the distance a person keeps from those around them. In the way they talk and act.

Scars can, too, be entirely invisible. They can be covered with a blanket of repression, felt like a princess's pea. A niggling stab in the heart of night's held breath. The sun may shine, but it's simply the darkness hiding behind a mask of smiles.

Every so often, when the wind blew chill or rain clouds threatened, Wendy rubbed her arm. She couldn't be sure if it was still painful from when she broke it as a young girl, but there was a definite ache.

Or the shadow of one.

She clenched her fist, then flexed her fingers to try to relieve the gnawing that might not have actually been really there. Wendy knew it was probably her imagination. She'd tried to forget the incident and others like it, but her memory, much better than she'd led Officer 'Call me Ravendra' Patel to believe, had a habit of bringing it to the surface occasionally.

She didn't want her guests to see her suffering. She couldn't do with the mutterings of sympathy or the offered hands wishing to help. She had to be seen as the genial host. Her 'mostest' couldn't be diminished. She wouldn't let it be.

She walked to her front room and looked out of the window at the park beyond. The Peoples' Park, to give it its proper title, was a large space housing a lake with swans, ducks and a fountain. On Wendy's side, there was a children's play area, bandstand and a wide grassy area where picnics were had, dogs ran and families did whatever families did.

Wendy felt the familiar pangs of envy or regret, she wasn't sure which, seeing a little girl running towards her parents, walking slightly ahead of her. Just as the girl reached them, the father spun around, scooped her up and threw her into the air, catching her again to squeals of delighted fright. She wrapped her arms around herself, mirroring the way the girl clung to her father. Her gaze moved down, seeing the way she held herself. She dropped her arms, the curse at being too sentimental quietly surfacing in her mind.

She pretended to ignore it and took a deep breath. She needed air. Or rather, she fancied some fresh air to blow away the cobwebs from being inside for too long, looking after her guests. Pulling on a light cardigan, she poked her head into the dining room.

"I'm just popping out for a few minutes. Would anyone like me to bring them something back? The ice cream man will be coming soon. I could get you a 99. A chocolate flake makes everything taste better, doesn't it?"

The occupants of the room didn't answer. Didn't look. Didn't move. She sighed. They didn't have to be so rude!

"Well, suit yourself. He has nuts and hundreds and thousands. You're missing out."

Still, she was ignored. She shrugged.

"I won't be long," she said.

She wasn't going to beg them. If they wanted to be ignorant, let them. She was going to all this trouble, only to be ignored. Her best China. Tea brewed to perfection. *Custard creams*, in fact.

"Hush now, Wendy," she told herself. "Stop being an old grump."

She knew she was right. She was tired and not a little stressed. She'd never, usually, be so judgemental. Maybe she needed the walk more than she'd care to admit. From the umbrella stand just beside the coat rack, she pulled out her walking stick. It was mahogany dark, with a trio of carved grooves spiralling down a third of its length. The handle was curved to fit her hand and the whole thing had a feeling of sturdiness. It would take her weight, which she was ashamed to admit was increasing too quickly for her liking, easily. It was also a capable club and, due to its smooth varnished surface, was easy to clean.

Today, however, nobody would need to be afraid of their skulls being cracked. Wendy just wanted a walk. A quick stroll around the park to get herself in order. Then she could see to her guests with the smile on her face genuine rather than forced.

The sun was behind her house when she stepped out of the front door, creating a shadow that seemed to not be concerned it was actually a nice day. It held the warmth at bay, not allowing it to venture into the darkened area, and Wendy shivered. She wasn't cold, but the difference between what she'd expected the temperature to be and what it really was, was so profound she was unprepared. Once she'd stepped out into the sun, however, she realised she should have left her cardigan inside. The sun pushed itself through her layers to banish the chill and wrap its arms around her. Instantly, she felt better.

She took a deep breath again, letting it out slowly. Closing her front garden gate, she crossed the road and was in the park grounds.

Wendy and Arthur had bought the house because of its proximity to such a place of natural beauty. Arthur always told his wife the park would always be jealous of her, because she'd always be prettier. In the town, not known for being picturesque, the Peoples' Park seemed out of place. Arthur and Wendy liked that. It made Wendy feel more at home and, if she was happy, he was.

Though there were a number of paths leading into the grounds, few people used them. They weren't laid close to where most visitors parked their cars, so were only really useful to those who walked there. Most stepped over the low railing and walked across the grass. Doing so took you through the tall trees. It took you past thick bushes.

It took you into areas beautiful and uplifting during the day, but dangerous by night.

When the dark fell and families left along with the light, the park became a haven for addicts and those wanting secret trysts in a place even the police kept clear of.

The descent of the park had happened only in recent years. In its almost entire 140 year history, it had been treated mostly with respect. Nowadays, Wendy was sure, respect also went home with the ending of the day.

The walk into the park was only short, so Wendy always took her time. The foliage dampened the noise of the world outside, both mentally and actually, and she enjoyed the sense of being enveloped by its blanket. It was a gradual effect that most wouldn't see, but she tried to always take notice of the little things.

The smile on the little boy doing forward rolls (or roly polies, as she was sure the young child would know them as). The tired, stressed look of the father contrasted by the calm, relaxed smile of the mother. The group of girls clustered in front of the bandstand, almost all staring into their mobile phone screens and none talking to each other. They wore makeup too grown up for their obvious youth, and showed too much flesh for Wendy's liking. The one girl who wasn't lost in her social media world was gazing across the grassed area. A group of boys were on their bicycles, with one foot on the ground to support them while three of their number smoked cigarettes. One kept glancing over at the girls. Wendy didn't find it too difficult to see where both were looking,

A dog had just left a gift for its owner on the grass near a bench. The owner tied the lead to the bench and attempted to pick up the present. It appeared he was having some troubles, however. It wasn't as firm as it could have been. A swan drifted across the water seemingly sleeping. Did they do that? Float whilst asleep? Wendy wished she could do that, except she'd be on an inflatable and it would be a swimming pool in a hotel in the sun. Or would have been twenty years ago. She was too old for such things now. She could only reminisce and sigh.

"It's a good life," said a young man.

He was tall and slim and wore simple jeans, paired with a plain polo necked t-shirt. His trainers were once white. They weren't dirty, Wendy noticed, but wore their age with pride. Scuffed and marked from a life of being comfortable and favoured whilst not entirely being cared for.

"Being a swan?" Wendy asked.

She felt no anxiety with talking to strangers. Arthur would tell her they were just friends she hadn't met yet. He said the same for the gang who'd stolen his watch and wallet when he left the Wheatsheaf on one of his rare nights out for a pint and a quiz. He hadn't been shaken, he believed it was a part of modern life, but he *did* like that watch. He'd bought a replacement, but didn't often wear it. It didn't feel like his old one. It didn't tell the time as well, he'd say.

"Yeah," the man said. "You just swim, sleep and scoff the bits of bread us lot throw at you."

"I suppose they do have it easy, if you put it like that."

"Hmmm."

The man was watching the swan intently. Wendy wondered if he wished he could swap places with the bird. She'd prefer staying as she was. Swans couldn't make tea, she thought. A day wasn't complete without a good brew.

She looked from the man back to the bird, but her eyes snapped back. His hand was balled in a fist. As first, she'd assumed it to be a natural curve of a relaxed hand, but then she saw he was gripping something. She moved, trying to make it look as if she wasn't staring. As he looked towards her, she returned her own eyes to the bird, as if she'd been watching it all along.

But she hadn't. He wasn't wishing he was the bird. He was jealous of it. Or had no feelings other than a desire to cause pain. The rock in his hand was held tightly enough for a sharp edge to draw blood. She could see it seeping through his fingers.

Wendy turned to him.

"You've cut yourself," she said, pointing.

He blushed, but his voice was even as he brought his hand up.

"Oh, damn," he said. "I didn't notice."

There was no reason given for the piece of stone to be held. None was needed, each knew the other was fully aware.

"I live just over there," Wendy said, gesturing. "Would you like a plaster?"

"No. I'm OK. It'll be fine."

"Don't be silly," she told him. "You don't want it getting infected."

The man looking from Wendy to the swan and back again. He did so twice more before speaking.

"Thanks," he said, dropping the rock by his feet. "Go on then."

"Come on," Wendy said, smiling. "I'll make you a nice cup of tea, too."

7 THEN

Wendy's arm took time to heal. Her parents gave her that time, but it came with the required insults and comments.

"You should have been more careful."

"That's what you get for flashing your bits to all those boys."

"Man up."

"Slut."

At school, things were just as bad. She was now a bigger laughing stock than before. She'd allowed one of her fellow classmates, a girl called Silvia, to sign the cast on her arm. It started out well enough, but the '*Get well*' was followed, to cheers of those surrounding them, by '*never, loser!!*'

Her arm wasn't the only casualty of the event. Her dignity suffered a similar break. Wendy had gone from someone the boys would barely speak to, to the girl they all wanted to see. Or, at least, see certain parts of her. It was now seemingly fine for her to be groped in the halls. She had to fend off whispers of 'Show us your tits.' She had to stop going to the toilet. That was, however, until the day she was so desperate for the toilet and so desperate *not* to go, she wet herself on her way home. She was sure she'd be able to hold it, but the impact of her feet on the paving slabs as she ran as fast as she could, shook her bladder to bursting point.

So, it burst in the only way it knew how.

Luckily, when she arrived home, her father was out and her

mother was asleep. She had time to change her clothes and hide the wet ones in the bottom of the laundry basket, plus make her mum a cup of tea before the woman awoke.

Wendy realised she couldn't be taking such risks. She might not get away with arriving home in piss-wet clothes a second time. Worse, potentially, was the fact she might have a similar accident while still at school. Not only would everyone there know, but she'd still have to go home and face her parents' wrath.

She would have to put up with the abuse.

Entrepreneurs can start their careers quite early in their lives. Money making schemes can drop into the heads of children like coins into their piggy banks. Often, such ideas come to the most unintelligent, belligerent bullies a school has to offer. On the times, as rare as she could make them, that Wendy did venture to the toilet, she would be followed. At first, it was Richard. Richie, he liked to be called. Richie Pullet. He could pull any girl, he'd joke, though his success with the opposite sex was mainly mythical rather than legendary.

Richie saw her go into the girls' toilets while he was on his way to the Principal's office for the second time that week. It was close to the end of the lesson, but his teacher refused to take any more of his disruption. He saw her enter and the idea was there, fully formed, right in front of him. He couldn't help but smile. He took up a position in front of the toilet's door.

The bell rang and children filled the halls. There was a twenty-minute break before the next lesson. Plenty of time.

"It's broken," he said to the first girl who wanted to use the facilities.

"What do you mean?"

"I mean," Richie said, sneering, "it's *broken*."

"All of them?"

"Every one. You'll have to go to the sports hall bogs."

"God, do I have to?"

"That's what Peterson said. I'm just here to make sure these ain't used."

Adam Peterson was one of the maths teachers and was well known to have a short temper. The girl shrugged and walked off.

"Rich," yelled Ozzie, Richie's best friend from a few feet away. Richie beckoned him over. "What you doing hanging around outside the girl's bogs?"

"Making money," Richie told him. "And you're gonna help."

"I like the sound of that."

"Good. Give me your... Fuck off."

The expletive was to a couple of girls who were deep in conversation and hadn't noticed the boy blocking their way into the toilets. They both stared at him before turning and walking away without a word, their conversation ceased.

Richie returned his attention to his friend. He needed to be quick.

"Stay here," he said quietly. "If you see any of our mates, tell them they'll get a nice surprise if they pay you a quid and come in here."

"A quid? What are they paying for?"

"Tits!"

"Woah!" exclaimed Ozzie. "How are they gonna see that? I wanna look!"

"You can go next time," Richie assured him. "Let's see how it goes. But they've got to keep it quiet. Just choose a couple for now. We can try more next time maybe."

Ozzie nodded.

"And then I get my shot?"

"Yeah. Maybe even cop a feel."

Ozzie smiled broadly.

"Who's are they?"

"Who do you think?" Richie said, winking. He made a diving motion with his hands.

Ozzie's eyes opened wide, but Richie had moved into the toilets before Ozzie could say anything else.

By the time the bell had gone to return to lessons, three boys had paid their money, two girls had been turned away and Wendy had been humiliated. She tried to object and to push past Richie, but he was too strong and his promise to tell everyone she'd shown him a lot more kept her scream to a whimper.

Wendy kept spare underwear and a skirt in her bag after the third time this had happened. She resisted the need to urinate, and so having a couple of accidents, and attempted to go to different toilets. Richie had tracked her down each time. And each time she'd spent the afternoon fighting back tears. Fighting the urge to run. Fighting the need to do Richie some serious damage.

When Wendy put off relieving herself long enough for her bladder to give way in the middle of Chemistry, her parents were called.

The girl was questioned about why she didn't ask to be excused, and why she didn't go at the recent break, but she refused to speak. She could have named her tormentors, but she'd pay for their punishment when they next saw her.

Her parents didn't take kindly to her reticence. Nor the accident in the first place. They did wait until they were home, parading as caring, disappointed and responsible parents in the principal's office. Home was another matter. Home was where societal rules didn't apply. Not unless her mother and father said so, anyway.

"How dare you embarrass us like that," her mother sneered, leaning into Wendy's face.

Her father didn't speak. He just slapped her. Hard. Twice.

8 THEN

Wendy learned not to cry.

Tears were the visible signs that her parents' treatment was working. Tears were their trophies, held high with smug sneers and the sharp cuts of words. Wendy didn't want them to enjoy themselves. She didn't want them to know it affected her. As she learned to hold the tears and feelings back, they began to be covered by the mental swallowing down of emotions. They were dulled. Smothered.

Wendy could still smile, but the warmth behind it cooled, then chilled.

One birthday, her parents bought her a hamster.

"We thought it'd do you good to look after something that doesn't do as it's told and just ignores you."

Wendy smiled, partly because she noticed how little the comment affected her, but mostly because she now, finally had a friend. A real one that would love her as much as she loved it. A real one who wouldn't laugh at accidentally exposed breasts or urine stains.

"What do you say?" her mother asked, tersely.

"Thank you," Wendy said

She meant it. Maybe her parents did actually think something of her.

She didn't give her new pet a name. None of those she thought of seemed to sit right on its diminutive shoulders. She decided it would simply be referred to as *'hamster'* or *'her.'* The hamster wouldn't mind, she thought. It might already have a name, but couldn't impart that knowledge to the girl. She didn't want to offend it by calling the animal something completely wrong.

Wendy was fastidious about cleaning out *her* cage. She wanted there to be no excuse for her parents to be angry or to complain, which would make them angry anyway. The hamster was fed and watered regularly. She didn't want *her* to have any excuse to not love her new owner.

For three weeks, all was well. Three weeks of smiles that were held internally lest they be taken as being secretive or deceitful. Or, even, deemed that Wendy was *happy*.

It seemed strange to Wendy to feel happy at all. She thought it was something that only happened to others. Her family life was permanently tainted, but that was her normal. She knew nothing else. For happiness to have seeped in implied her normal was actually temporary.

Or could be.

Three weeks.

Then the hamster escaped.

She didn't notice immediately. She'd shut the cage, as always. She knew she had. *Surely* she had. Wendy wasn't the sort of girl who made such mistakes. She didn't want the hamster getting hurt, and really didn't want to anger her parents. So where was she? Why wasn't she there, running endlessly on her wheel, or asleep on her bed, or shitting in her corner? Why was the cage door slightly open?

Wendy felt the rise of panic within her, feeling unsure whether it was purely concern or if the turmoil in her stomach and pull at her throat was impending vomit. She swallowed it back down, either way. The most important thing to do was find *her*. Find her before anyone else did.

She dropped to her knees to begin hunting under her bed and behind her chest of drawers. She pulled back the curtains that were long enough to brush the carpet when drawn. Wendy always kept her bedroom tidy anyway, of course, so hiding places *should* have been at a minimum. Still, the hamster was only small and could probably fit in spaces smaller than seemed possible.

Then she heard the swearing from her father.

She knew where the hamster was.

Resisting the urge to run, she walked as calmly as she could through to the living room. Her father was standing in the middle of the room with his arms folded. Her mother was crouched in front of him, cleaning up a number of small, elongated pellets. The hamster hadn't just escaped to the lounge, it had used the floor as a toilet.

Wendy gulped and could feel herself begin to shake. She tried to internalise the tremble to the point where she could feel her teeth rattle against each other.

Neither parent looked at her. Her father handed his wife a piece of cucumber, and the woman started to make tutting sounds, offering out the cucumber slice to entice the animal out. It was a tactic Wendy had used many times in her room, so it was one that was bound to work. And it did. Within a few seconds, the hamster ran out from under the sofa. It stopped, sniffed, rubbed its snout and scampered on, straight to where Wendy's mother had placed the cucumber.

On the carpet where the animal had defecated.

Wendy stopped walking as her mother stood and stepped back.

"What have we told you about this thing being kept in your room?" her father said evenly. "What have we said about making sure it only shit in its cage?"

Wendy remained silent. She didn't believe an answer was required. Giving one would have betrayed her anxiety and could easily fuel the fire in the man's belly. She did, however, nod.

"What did we say would happen if you messed up?"

Wendy thought about it, but couldn't recall such a conversation. She knew, if her pet *did* get out of her room, there'd be consequences, so no such talk had been required.

"I..." she began, not knowing where the sentence would lead.

She didn't have the chance to find out.

Her father's foot swung back, then forward. There was a shriek from the animal, echoed by Wendy, as the foot impacted with a force that would probably have broken the ribs and spine of the hamster. The thud as it hit the wall just above the television would have ensured any previously lethal damage was now fatal.

Wendy's hamster and only real friend fell, landing on the unit the television was standing on.

"Pass it to me," her father said.

Wendy ran to where the animal lay, unmoving. Carefully, she lifted it, cradling it to her chest. No tears flowed, but she could feel something break inside of her.

"Give the bloody thing here," ordered her father.

Wendy knew she had to do as he said, but didn't want to give up her friend. She wished she'd given *her* a name. She realised the hamster wouldn't have really minded.

"Now!"

She hadn't realised she'd hesitated, and jumped at the sudden sound. Moving as quickly as her father's tone demanded, she complied.

"I knew this thing was a mistake," he said. "You can't even look after yourself, let alone an animal or this... *rodent*."

He said the word as if he was calling it something far worse. Wendy flinched at the inflection, wanting to defend *her* but not having the courage to. A layer of guilt settled on her sorrow, darkening it and giving a weight that was almost smothering.

Her father, though she longed to be able to say 'you're not my real dad!', walked through to the kitchen. He pressed the pedal on the bin that was tucked in the space between the fridge and the wall. As it wasn't emptied as often as it should be, there was a constant (and constantly ignored) fusty, decaying odour when you opened the refrigerator door. The bin was as full as usual, the contents gripping the top edge as if waiting for the lid to open so they could launch themselves into freedom, but stopped when they saw who had lifted the lid.

Wendy had followed him and watched as he held the dead hamster by the tip of its tail, flicked it to watch the animal swing, then let go. The hamster dopped onto the pile of used tea bags and beer bottles with a sound far too flat to represent the pleasure Wendy had felt while it was her pet.

Her father walked away, the pedal's release allowing the lid to settle back down. It didn't quite sit flush with the top of the bin, the hamster's body causing it to be raised slightly.

"Bed." her father said as he re-entered the living room. With a final look at the bin's lid and a final whisper of love to her friend, she went to bed. As she passed her parents, neither acknowledged her.

I'll see you again, Wonder, she thought, giving the animal the first name that came to her. *You'll never leave me again.*

9 THEN

Sleep can be elusive. When your mind wars against you, using flashes of memory as weapons to stab at your mind with grief and fear and regret, you can become a wanderer on the battlefield. You cling to your closed eyes like a shield, knowing it is futile. The onslaught is too much. You will not, can never, win.

Wendy tried. Wendy failed.

What her father had done was a bubbling mess of clenched cheeked diarrhoea churning in her stomach. Though she'd eaten nothing out of the ordinary, the urge to defecate was becoming harder to resist, but the girl still refused to go to the toilet. She felt she should punish herself for allowing *her* to be killed in such a way. In *any* way.

Her tummy growled at her in protest and she had no choice but to submit to its warnings. The retribution from her parents for soiling her bedding was something she preferred to not think about. It was better to mourn than mess.

Quietly, she went into the bathroom and evacuated her bowels. She liked that phrase. It made her feel like Howard Carter discovering the tomb of Tutankhamun. Egyptian history and mythology were something Wendy had been interested in for as long as she could remember, and she could think of few things better than the joy of such a discovery. She would happily rake through sand and dirt in excessive heat to bring new treasures to the world.

And speaking of raking through dirt…

Wendy peeked through the sliver of a gap in the door to the living room. Both of her parents had fallen asleep in front of the television. A gameshow she had never seen before was still on, with the host making the audience and contestants laugh at jokes she didn't understand.

She knew the door opened fairly smoothly, but pushed it slowly anyway. She didn't want this to be the first time it decided to creak as it opened, a yawning, just woken up, jaw ready to call out her appearance to her slumbering parents. The door kept her secret and allowed her to slip into the room silently.

Her mother was lolling forwards in her usual seat. Her chin was on her neck, though she was slumped down into the cushions, a position Wendy thought should have caused her head to roll back. The woman was snoring, though it wasn't loud enough to drown out the noise from the television. Her father was next to his wife. His hand was on her lap and his head on her shoulder. He wasn't snoring, but seemed to be mumbling in his sleep. Wendy had no intention of moving closer to find out what that might be.

Timing her footsteps to coincide with bursts of laughter and cheers from the game show, the girl made her way into the kitchen. She hesitated at the bin. The hamster was in there. Dead. Would it be dining on the ghosts of the other food scraps that were in there with it? Mostly eaten pizza slices. Old tea bags. An odd tin of beans that hadn't been fully emptied out. Did dead animals eat dead food? Ghost devouring ghost?

Wendy smiled at the thought. She knew, or extremely doubted, it would happen, but the thought was interesting. Still smiling, she lifted the bin lid and, with a sense of wonder, picked up Wonder. She wasn't worried about the hamster's absence being noticed. She was the one who would have to empty the bin to take the rubbish out anyway, and it would need doing in the morning before school, so there was little chance of her pet's disappearance being noticed.

She returned to her room with the same prowess she'd displayed on the first journey.

"We're back together, now Wonder," she whispered once her bedroom door was closed. "He won't hurt you again."

Wonder, the deceased rodent, didn't reply, but Wendy knew she'd heard her.

Looking around her room, she chose an old shoe box that held her pens and felt tips. Taking the lid off, she emptied its contents on the bed, keeping her hand over the pens to quieten their noise. The pens fitted easily into one of the drawers set into the base of her divan. With some tissue and toilet roll, Wonder could be laid out to rest. As least until she wanted to bring her out again.

She had yet to really think through what she was doing with the hamster formally known as simply *her*. Her father had killed her only real friend, and she wanted that friend back. The fact Wonder was still dead and, obviously, would remain so, was not lost on the girl, but she didn't dwell on it. Life and death were still a mystery to her. She knew the basics – you were born, lived and died. From the moment you are born, her mother had once told her, you are dying. Wendy disagreed. Medically, that might be the truth, but she wouldn't think of it like that. She was living so she would live.

That life had, she believed, started with Wonder. She would ensure it continued. It was a pretence, but one she was comfortable with. No one knew what happened after death, so she was able to believe what she wanted. Or pretend it, at least.

So, for her, Wonder was dead, but could still be her friend.

After dark was her favourite time. She'd be shut in her room, away from any chance to annoy her parents. Summer had been left behind by the ongoing march of Time, and had passed the baton of seasonal janitorship over to Autumn. The sun was becoming tired of lighting the day for so long, so gave in to the whisperings of the moon. *'Let me take over,'* Wendy imagined Lunar saying. *'I'll keep everything safe for you.'* She didn't blame the sun for being tired. It had the whole solar system to light. The moon only had the little planet imaginatively called Earth to illuminate. She had energy to spare.

In the faded light of the moon or her dimmed lamp, Wonder didn't look dead. She was asleep, a sleep she couldn't be roused from. She must have been having a *wonder*ful dream. Maybe she was hunting bad parents and stomping on them with giant shoes that somehow fitted the animal's tiny feet. Perhaps she was dreaming that she was dreaming, and in that dream, she was dreaming. A rabbit – or hamster – hole of never-ending dreams. What if death was actually that? A spiral of slumbering imaginings taking you forever into the lost abyss of your mind?

Wendy had that and similar conversations with her hamster night after night. Long after she should be asleep, she was still holding and stroking the pet. At least until decomposition began. She noticed the signs appearing after the first week. Wonder had become stiff, then bloated. And she smelled. Wendy tried to keep her bedroom windows open, even though the weather didn't want to remain suitable for such ventilation. Air fresheners didn't help either. She tried to ignore it and, when confronted by her father, she apologised and told him she'd forgotten to shower.

"For a month?" he'd asked.

She didn't answer, but knew she needed to find another home for Wonder if she wanted to keep her. Though she put it off a couple of days, the appearance of the maggots told her she could wait no longer.

10 NOW

Lee, as the man introduced himself, didn't really drink tea, but would make an exception on this occasion. Two sugars, please, and not much milk. No, no biscuits, thanks.

Once tea was made and served, Wendy took Lee into the front lounge and told him to sit down on the sofa.

"Lovely view out there, isn't it?" she asked, pointing to the large netted window.

Lee nodded. It wasn't bad. You could see the park. A squirrel ran up a tree, which caused him to smile. Of course, you also had to deal with noisy kids playing and dog owners who didn't clean the crap up after their dogs had left it behind from their behind.

Wendy took his hand in hers and removed the tea towel she'd originally given hm when they entered her house. She saw him look around. Interest? Too much? She berated herself. Just because he'd held that stone with intent, didn't mean his eyes held just as much.

The stone had dug into the flesh on opposite sides of his palm, framing it in bloody tears.

"It doesn't really hurt," Lee insisted.

"I know," Wendy said. *You're so big and strong, I bet you think nothing can hurt you*, she thought. *And you think you can hurt anything else.*

"Have your tea," she told him. "I'll go get my first aid kit. It'll need cleaning out or it could get infected."

Lee looked concerned at that. Wendy smiled to herself, keeping her mouth tight enough to not let it stray to her features.

"Don't worry," she told him. "Before I retired, I was a nurse. I know exactly what I'm doing."

Lee relaxed. A sweet old lady who was once a nurse? She'd sort his hand out in no time. It was stinging, he had to admit. The stone was sharper than he'd expected, and this *Wendy* showing up had spoiled his fun. The past week or two had been rough, what with that bitch of a girlfriend dumping him and his arsehole boss sacking him. It was only a bit of weed. A couple of bottles. He hadn't hurt anyone with the fork lift. Just damaged a car or two. The swan had been sitting there looking all pretty and condescending. It was laughing at him. Showing its superiority. Well, he would show who was superior. Who was boss.

Except, instead of being stoned being the problem, a stone had put an end to his self-pitied attack.

Once the woman had fixed his hand, he'd excuse himself to use her toilet. Then he'd fleece her. Old people were no good at hiding valuables. He knew all the places to look and could do so in less time than it would take a grown man to piss. He'd be all gracious and thankful, and she would be none the wiser.

He was staring into his tea, his mind wandering through the possible rooms upstairs and what treasures they might reveal. He didn't hear Wendy walk back into the lounge or slowly up behind him. By the time he felt the pinch of the needle in his neck, its payload had already been administered. The deed was done. Any reaction he might have had would be short lived.

And it was.

"Shit!" he managed to say, pulling away, but that was all. His eyes were closed before he fell to the floor.

"Such bad language!" Wendy exclaimed.

She picked up the cup from where Lee had dropped it and took it back to the kitchen. When she returned, she was carrying a roll of kitchen tissue and a spray. She bent, pulled the trigger of the spray bottle and aimed at the discarded tea, carefully dabbing up the liquid.

"There," she said eventually. "Good as new."

Wendy looked down at the man, sadly. They just didn't fall well. It was never a simpleaning back of the head, or perhaps a slip to the side. They'd be forward, off the sofa. An awkward angle or their arms trapped under them. How inconsiderate.

She'd deal with Lee in a little while. First, she still had her own cup of tea to finish and she also needed a few things from the local supermarket. The tea bag tin wouldn't fill itself, more's the pity! She had plenty of time. Though he wasn't quite dead yet, he probably would be by the time she got back. It'd save waiting around for it to happen. She did so dislike having to wait.

11 THEN

The quietest of places can seem so full of noise, you can feel crushed under its cacophony. When the voices of doubt, reason and guilt are vying for their chance to speak out, their words stumble over one another in the stampede of introspection.

Yet, in the busiest cities of the world, with their herds of migrating tourists and head down, coffee drinking, phone swiping office workers rushing to catch their bus or train or taxi, it's possible to stand for a moment. To close your eyes. To breathe.

At least until someone jostles you and swears because it's your fault they weren't watching where they were going.

But, even that once moment of peace, you exist. You *are*.

For Wendy, that place was Bradley Woods. A large, at least to the local populace, forest, Bradley Woods was an oft used area for dog walkers and family picnickers. And night time drug addicts. And weekend doggers of a different variety.

It was also home to a small stream. The water way was meagre even in months where heavy rainfall drenched the area, but this small stream seemed to only be able to handle a small amount of the liquid that did its best to give the shallow cleft a name. It started in a dip caused by the lightning struck uprooting of a fledgling oak tree. With perhaps the only actual influx of rainwater that particular location had ever encountered, the stream was born. For Wendy and many others, the fallen tree was a rough but serviceable seat. For Wendy, however, an area further into the forest was more inviting.

Just past the end of the tree, the part that had been reaching for the stars when Nature decided to cut its life and length short, the forest became denser. At first, it was only slightly. Over the several hundred years of the Woods' existence, every inch of it had been traversed or explored. More by intrepid children than curious adult, but there was little that was still untouched. In more recent times, this exploration had diminished. People were too busy to venture off the well beaten paths, however much their dogs might wish to. Children would delve slightly into its depths, but not too far. You never knew who was hiding in places you couldn't see.

Wendy wasn't as concerned. The treatment she received from her parents had numbed her to potential dangers somewhat. She was aware strangers could mean dangers, but felt they could be no worse than her mother and father. She wore gloves to avoid scratches on her hands, a change of clothes in a carrier bag and moved *slowly*.

That's how the girl found her quiet place.

It was the barest of clearings. A held breath in the growth of the forest. A skipped heartbeat in its long life. Surrounded by tall, old trees and with gaps stuffed with bushes and branches, it allowed only the stream passage through. And Wendy. She wasn't concerned with carving her name into bark or pulling leaves off and dropping them to the floor. She wouldn't step on crawlies she didn't find creepy. She wanted only to be able to breathe.

There, she could. There, she took Wonder. She thought of burying her friend, but couldn't bring herself too. What if the creature woke up, or the ghost did, and found itself smothered by mud? How would Wendy, herself, feel?

No.

She built a small nest from twigs and leaves, apologising to the trees and hoping they'd understand, and placed it carefully in a slight depression in the ground not far from the stream. It should be sheltered enough from the elements and any prying eyes. Though the water level was hardly more than a mouthful of spit at that time, Wonder would have enough to drink if needed.

She stayed with her friend for a little while, but knew she needed to get home quickly if she wanted to keep any parental reprimands to a minimum.

"I need to go, Wonder," she said quietly. She stroked the hamster's back, then picked out an emerging maggot and threw it away. "I'll be back soon."

The 'soon' was, unfortunately, four days later. Wendy had tried her best to return the very next day, but parents and homework and a visit to the hospital A&E department due to the mug that fell out of the cupboard and hit her on her head *(make sure you keep to the story!)*, causing a cut and a large lump, delayed her. In that time, it had rained on one day and there'd been a flash heatwave lasting two days. Wendy hoped neither had been too uncomfortable for her pet. When she finally returned, she saw the weather was the least of Wonder's problems.

The decay had accelerated, or perhaps, in her inexperience of such things, Wendy had underestimated its speed. The hamster's body had deflated, though it was being feasted upon by myriad bugs and flies that gave it the appearance of bulk. She shooed the insects away and scooped some of the stream's water, which the rain had replenished, to wash the remains clean of any remaining diners. A quick flick or two forced the departure of the odd straggler.

She stepped back and turned away to wipe her hands on leaves to remove the dirty feeling that clung to them and, when she looked back, a fox was creeping towards the carcass.

"Get away!" she shouted, stamping her foot at the animal. "Leave her alone!"

The fox ran off into the forest, leaving Wendy to see, possibly for the first time, what had become of her pet. She had been looking past the death and all it brought, seeing only the beauty of the friend she'd had. The friend she'd now lost.

Well, the body needed disposing of, but Wonder's spirit would remain. She could come back here and still be close to *her*. No one, not even her father, could take that away. She picked up the physical remains, wrapping the leaves from the nest around it, and held it in her hands. She closed her eyes.

"Sweet dreams," she said.

It was a simple gesture that didn't convey all Wonder had meant to her, but it wasn't something she'd have been able to put into words anyway. It was done, then. She closed her hands and squeezed, crushing the small body in her not much larger hands. The crunch of bones was oddly satisfying. The squelch from the now liquified innards made her smile. It sounded as if Wonder was farting her own goodbye.

She threw the mess of nest and body beyond the clearing's perimeter. It didn't need to be there anymore. It had done its job and now could be food for whatever wished to consume it. Wendy could still feel the hamster's presence, and that was what mattered.

12 THEN

In school, friends can often be far from anything resembling that title. Children of all ages can be so desperate to fit in, to be liked, they will accept the illusion of friendship when the reality seems such an impossible ideal. They don't conform. They wear glasses. They're heavier than the pretty, popular kids. Acne. Hair colour. Name. The ammunition for those who wish to arm themselves with insults and the ability to cause physical and mental pain is freely available, as if spawned by a galactic game of C.O.D.

Wendy wanted friends. Not necessarily even a plural amount. Just one would do. She'd tried to remain an outsider, but that had not worked. She'd tried to follow the will of those who said they liked her and had fallen foul of their mistreatment. She didn't know which way to go. When Pagan approached her, Wendy immediately looked for an avenue of escape. She saw one, the corridor that led towards the science block, and started to walk towards it, trying to act as if that was obviously the way she wanted to go. Her next lesson was in the other direction, but she could turn left at Chemistry and go around the back of the school canteen.

"Wendy!" Pagan called after her.

Wendy ignored the shout, acting as if she hadn't heard it. She did, however, speed up her pace. Pagan started to run and was beside her before she'd reached the corridor.

"Where are you going to so fast? Didn't you hear me shout you?"

Wendy looked confused.

"No," she said. "Was miles away."

"I just wanted to say sorry for all that stuff at the pool. I didn't mean to."

"You didn't mean to humiliate me?"

"No!" Pagan shook her head emphatically. "Well, maybe, but I didn't want you to be that humiliated. Just, you know, a bit."

"Is that supposed to make me feel better?"

"No, of course not, I'm just apologising, that's all. Don't make it hard for me."

"Why shouldn't I?" asked Wendy, unsure if the bravado she was faking was the right thing to do. She didn't want to anger the girl, just make her squirm a bit.

"Because…" Pagan paused and looked around before continuing. "Look, my dad told me I had to say sorry."

"So, you're doing this because you've been told to? That means you don't mean it, so it doesn't count."

"No, I mean yes, but I was going to do it anyway."

"OK."

Wendy turned and made to step away, but Pagan held her arm.

"I do mean it," she said. "I was only messing. Trying to make you stronger, like one of us."

"One of you? Why would I want that?"

Did she want that, Wendy thought. The answer was easy. Yes, she really thought she did. One of them. One of the gang.

"You want to be in our group? We'll prove it to you."

"You're only going to make…"

"I'm not, honest. Come on, it'll be fun."

Wendy thought about the offer. If she took it, she might just be made to feel inferior and foolish. She might, however, have the promised fun. She might be accepted. If she declined, it would add to the pile of ammunition the school bullies had. Pagan would be pissed off and everyone would know why. The freak didn't want to be liked.

"OK."

"Cool," said Pagan, smiling broadly.

"So… now what?"

"Now, you're in the group."

"That's it?"

"What else did you expect? We don't have weird initiation rights. I don't want you to open a vein or wear a cone on your head."

Wendy laughed and saw Pagan smile. The girl was beautiful. Why couldn't *she* look like that?

"Right," said Pagan matter of factly. "First off are the rules. You're given one, follow it and you get another. There's only three, so it's nothing to worry about. Just to spice it up a bit."

"What are they?"

"You only find out the first one, first. You get the next after you've done that."

Wendy nodded. That was fair enough, though why have rules at all?

"We want to make sure everyone is committed to each other. If you don't make rules, you don't know if people are serious about it. Are you serious?"

Wendy nodded.

"I'm serious."

"Right. On the fourth Wednesday of the month, we don't wear underwear. No knickers or bra. It's about the freedom to be female without following what others tell us we've got to."

Wendy paled.

"No… No underwear?"

"Yep. Every fourth Wednesday. Only those in our group know, so there's no fear of anyone else finding out. It's like a dare, but it makes you feel powerful. It's weird. You up for it?"

Wendy wasn't sure. It sounded just like another chance for them to make fun of her. Who did that sort of thing at school?

"I don't know…?"

"Come on, don't be scared. We're friends now. Like I said, it's a way to make sure everyone can keep our secrets and are committed to each other. No biggie."

No biggie? Wendy thought it was very much a 'biggie'. Still, Pagan seemed to be telling the truth. It was a lot to ask of someone if the whole thing was just made up. Pagan's group wasn't particularly large, but they held a position of authority amongst the other children. You didn't cross them. If you did, you'd be set upon by all of them and the plenty of others who thought standing with them would cement their membership. You did as they told you, not asked, or you'd likely find your head being shoved into a soiled toilet bowl while it was flushed.

"Yeah?" Pagan prompted. She put her hand on Wendy's arm and squeezed it gently. "I'm trying to make up for being a bitch. Come on, say yes. I just figured being tough on you would make you stronger, you know?"

Wendy nodded. It sounded plausible, she thought, but she also wondered if that was because she wanted it to be. She didn't want it to be a lie.

"OK," she said. "I'd like that."

"Excellent!" Pagan exclaimed.

"When is the next fourth Wednesday?"

"Tomorrow!"

Tomorrow?

Shit.

"That OK?"

"Sure."

"Nice! I'll see you tomorrow."

"See you tomorrow."

Wendy had three more lessons that day, but couldn't remember any of them afterwards, not even English, which was her favourite. By the time she was running home, she struggled to remember anything about the day at all. Anything except the conversation with Pagan, that was.

No underwear. Did she dare? Was she being entirely stupid, or was Pagan being honest? She hoped it was the latter and went to sleep that night with her stomach in knots and her mind whirlpooling.

The next morning, she stood in front of her chest of drawers. The top drawer held her underwear. The various items were neatly laid out in even rows, with matching or almost matching garments next to each other. Wendy chose a set and put them on her bed beside her uniform. Her conversation with Pagan had been repeating in her mind from the moment she woke, and she had yet to decide which path she was going to take. Her stomach was more settled than it had been the night before, but she felt no less anxious. She had never even thought about leaving the house, or her bedroom for that matter, *commando*. Her hand hovered over the underwear before moving to her shirt. Then back again and yet again.

She couldn't, she knew, back out. Pagan and her group would make her life miserable. Or more miserable. The incident after the pool and in the bathroom had been awful, but she had managed to push past them. If the worst case happened, and Pagan was planning on embarrassing her, she would, yet again, get by. School didn't last a life time. After it was over, she never had to see any of the other children again. She could reinvent herself if she wished. But she could wish. She could hope. Tomorrow, a new life could be offering itself.

To grasp it, courage and risks had to be taken.

Wendy picked up her underwear and put it back in the drawer. She then proceeded to dress herself, pleased the school insisted on blazers being worn at all times, in all weathers. It hid obvious signs of being braless. She felt naked, even with the clothes.

Taking a deep breath, the girl gripped the door handle, turned it and pulled the door open.

13 THEN

Wendy walked to school slower than usual.

She was convinced all eyes were on her, though she knew she was being foolish. To everyone else, another school girl staring at the floor as she went was much the same as any other one on any other day. When she did look up and glance around her, no one was taking any notice. No one was watching or looking her way in passing. She was invisible as most were. Peoples' lives were too busy for them to take notice of a girl who appeared, particularly in uniform, almost a clone of all the rest.

Wendy wished that anonymity would last while she was at school. Nobody would see her. She'd simply go about her day, encountering no one and be able to go home unscathed. But she would have done it. Accepted the challenge and risen to it. She'd have joined the ranks of the school elite.

Unfortunately, that wasn't to be.

Pagan was waiting for her, stepping out from behind the large notice board that stood at the entrance to the school's playground. Her appearance made Wendy jump, which gave Pagan reason to both smile and take the advantage – not that she wouldn't have had it anyway.

"Hi Wendy," she said, smiling. "How are you? Did you sleep OK?"

Wendy smiled back, knowing it was fake and knowing the other girl would see it as such.

"Come on. Don't be scared. If you've done it, you're one of us. If you haven't, you're not. It's that simple. Up to you."

She was making it appear as if Wendy deciding to not go through with it was 'no biggie'. There'd be no recriminations. If only the possibility were true.

"So?" Pagan prompted.

At first, Wendy didn't say anything. She didn't know if she should admit to being naked beneath her clothes. Of course, she didn't have a choice and Pagan probably knew that. She had no time to decide as, suddenly, the pair were surrounded by the rest of the group she was so desperate to be a part of.

Rebecca, never Becky. Amanda. Boris, the girl whose name was a strange mix of letters that didn't go together, so was called Boris by everyone including the teachers and her own parents. Terry, Pagan's on-off boyfriend who only hung around to be at her beck and call, thinking that was the way to her heart. He didn't realise she thought he was an idiot, but he looked OK and wasn't a bad kisser. And he spent all his pocket money on her. Davina smelled like wet dog but had a rich father, and Caroline wanted to be Pagan when she grew up. There were others, but they were hangers on. There to bulk up the numbers and make the gang seem larger than it was. The core was the seven, including the boyfriend, but they had all arrived for the show.

They wore their outer clothing only, just as she did. They *did*. She had nothing to fear because this would be a bonding moment for them all. For once, she would belong.

Wendy nodded, a small, uneasy smile playing at the corners of her mouth.

"I did it," she said quietly.

"I knew you would!" Pagan exclaimed excitedly. "Come on, show us!"

"Well, can't we all do it together? You've all done it too, haven't you?"

"Of course,we have, them's the rules. But the new members always have to show us first. Otherwise they could have chickened out and we've got nothing to deny if they grass us up."

Wendy thought about it. Pagan made a good point. If they showed they weren't wearing anything under their uniform and it got out, they'd be in *so* much trouble. They needed to know new members of their group were being serious.

She took a deep breath.

She put her hand to her hip, preparing to pull the waistband of her skirt away. No way was she going to lift the hem and show everyone everything.

"Wait," said Pagan, smiling and putting her hand on Wendy's arm.

"Not like that. We have a special way."

Wendy dropped her hand. The smile was disarming and put her at ease. She was so close, she forgot about it maybe being a ploy.

"Terry, you're up."

"Huh?" Terry looked confused, as if he had no idea what he was supposed to do.

Confusion and fear tried to creep back into Wendy's mind, but she was still caught up in the possibility of being part of the group. She dismissed the doubt.

"Come on, check she's telling the truth."

"But… I… How?"

"Stick your hand up her blazer. Cop a feel. You'll be able to tell."

"I… I don't think I should."

"If you don't, you won't get hold of mine ever again."

Terry's glance to Wendy was one of apology and his own fear. You didn't say no to Pagan, whether she was promising things or not.

"You don't… don't need to," Wendy stammered, backing away.

She didn't get far, as the crowd that had grown from the main group to many more who just wanted to know what the fuss was about stopped her. Hands pushed her forwards towards the boy, causing her to bump into him and bounce back. Terry seemed to have come to terms with the situation and had an expression of expectant pleasure on his face. If he had to grope a girl's chest, he was going to enjoy it.

"You want to join us, right?" Pagan asked, continuing before Wendy could respond. "So this is how you do it."

Wendy used to have a crush on Terry, but that was a long time before. Since he'd become Pagan's lapdog after she'd finished with Thomas, he'd lost his most attractive quality – his confidence. Even if she still liked him in that way, she would certainly not want him touching her. She knew quite a few of the girls had gone further – much further in the case of Pagan, but she had no plans to do so herself.

"Don't," she pleaded to both Pagan and Terry. "Please."

"Awww," whined Pagan before laughing. "Does Wendy not like her boobies touched?" She looked at her boyfriend. "Now, Tez."

Terry nodded and moved forward, raising his hand in

preparation. Wendy thought desperately how to stop this from happening, and could think of only one.

She grabbed the hem of her skirt and lifted.

The sound that followed was a muddled mess of cheers, laughter and shrieks. Applause rippled under the noise like a low thunder and Wendy wished lightning would strike her. She was only then aware of just how many surrounded her. Until that moment, everyone else had faded into the background, with only Pagan and Terry existing. Now, the world had exploded in on her, bringing with it her shattered dignity and the terrible realisation.

She dropped her skirt and stared at Pagan. The other girl was holding her chest as she struggled to breath through the gasp of hilarity that shook her body.

"The stupid munt fell for it! Not Bendy Wendy ain't got any undies on!"

"But you said…"

"I never said anything, so don't try and pin this on me! You wanna go commando, you're on your own!"

She moved closer to the humiliated, again, girl. This couldn't have gone any better.

"Maybe you've done it to make sure you're *not* on your own, eh? Come on boys, she's begging for it!"

The cheers erupted again, louder this time. Wendy wrapped her arms around herself and barged through the throng. No one tried to stop her. Let her go. She'd have to come back, and this was one disgrace that wouldn't be forgotten. The girl was now a legend, in all the wrong ways.

14 NOW

The shopping experience can be divisive. There are those who hate it with a passion. The ones who order everything with Prime and are pissed if it takes more than a day to arrive. They book the slot for their shopping to be delivered and, when they step out of the house, have to emerge blinking into a world that has forgotten they exist beyond their constant data stream.

There are also those to whom holding the thing they are purchasing, touching it and seeing the physical object, is therapeutic. Whether it be a simple apple or television, a pack of toilet rolls or a dress for the really fancy dinner they are going to, they need to feel the new shiny thing they are going to hand over their cash (or swipe their card) for.

Wendy fell into the middle, somewhere. She had never used a computer, though she did own a smartphone. Online ordering of food was alien to her. She wanted to see the food, particularly the fruit, she was buying. She hadn't bought a new dress in too many years as, since her dear husband's passing, she'd had no reason to go anywhere that might need one. All her clothes were getting on in years, but were far from tatty. She kept all her garments in the best condition she could, and had been adept with a needle and thread since her youth. Age, hers rather than her clothes, was making her fingers dislike doing anything that required intricate work, but Wendy would not accept defeat just yet.

So, while she didn't dislike shopping or social interactions, she went when she needed to. It served a purpose and nothing more. She had everything she needed other than the essentials a trip to the supermarket would provide. For this visit, Wendy only wanted a few items, so she wouldn't be gone for too long. There was no need to rush, though. Lee wasn't going anywhere.

By the time she returned home, she expected him to be dead. Stopping to chat to a neighbour she hadn't seen for a few weeks had filled in a scattering of extra minutes, so there had been plenty of time for the poison to take effect.

She was surprised to see him still moving when she re-entered her lounge. There were only odd twitches and the occasional fluttering of his eyelids, but he wasn't completely gone yet.

"You're a fighter, aren't you? Well, maybe I should let that swan have a go at you now. See who would win that fight."

Casually, she took a cushion from the sofa and put it against the man's face. She pressed down. He didn't fight. He couldn't. Any control Lee might have had of his limbs had long since expired, just as the rest of him soon would.

And, then, it had. There wereno more twitches. His eyes remained closed, his body still.

"Good man," Wendy said, replacing the cushion on the sofa. "Now, would you like to join my friends and have a fresh tea?"

It took some effort, but eventually, Lee was sitting in the dining room with Wendy's other guests. She'd introduced him, but the others were as reticent with their greetings as ever. They were a private bunch, she thought. She didn't know why she put up with it, but she was a patient woman.

Besides, being dead, they would probably not really be in that much of a talkative mood.

She would drain his bodily fluids later when she'd mixed the home-made embalming fluid her husband had created. He had dabbled in taxidermy for a while, turning the garage they had in their old home into a workshop full of stuffed animals, carcases and animal hides that he didn't want to use after he'd skinned the creature. Spending some time in a funeral directors to satisfy a macabre interest in death, something Wendy found bizarre but oddly attractive, had given him the knowledge to preserve his trophies so well, they looked as if they could pounce from their mounts at any moment. It had also given him the means to permanently borrow, for the man would never steal, enough chemicals to keep his hobby going for long after he had lost interest.

Wendy, however, had found her own use for his legacy. She thanked her late husband on many occasions for providing her with the means to have friends.

She would usually have had a batch already prepared, but hadn't expected the surprise visitor to join her tea party.

How nice.

She would just apply a little make up, in the form of a thick decking varnish she used to clog the pores and orifices, thus extending the time before decomposition and disposal was required.

Wendy was far from experienced in such things. Albert, God rest his soul, if he had a soul, had never shown his wife the required methods. She mixed the snippets of conversations they'd had with guesswork to give her some semblance of a technique. It worked. Mostly.

She went to the kitchen to get her apron from the back of the pantry and opened a fresh pair of gloves. They were the same type she used to wash the pots though, for this, she always used new, never pre-worn. She owed her guests that.

Back in the room, she noticed Lee was leaning slightly to the side.

"Don't slouch, young man," she said, curtly. "It's rude and unbecoming. You won't get any biscuits with that behaviour."

She took hold of him under his arms and pulled him straight. The effort made her breathless and she had to lean against the wall for a moment to stop the vertigo she was suffering from more and more from sending her to the floor.

She admonished herself. Getting older did not mean becoming unfit. What good was she to her friends if she couldn't even lift them without almost passing out?

"I need a cup of tea," she said to the occupants of the room. "Would anyone else like one?"

She waited for an answer and, when none came, tutted.

"Don't all speak at once, you know. All this noise will give me a headache."

She looked around the room, slowly, and couldn't help smiling. They were all there, just for her. Friends. Guests. There were no swear words, which Wendy couldn't abide, or any untoward comments. Just a nice, peaceful and friendly tea party.

She went through to the kitchen to make the tea.

She sang while she moved, her voice high with a slight vibrato that once joined in with others to fill a church hall. The vibrato had become somewhat shakier as the years had progressed, but Wendy ignored that. She always sung when happy, and would continue to until either her voice, mind or life was gone.

In the back garden of her neighbour's house, Benjamin, the gent who'd lived there for the past three years with his two dogs and one cat, was sitting at his patio table. He was reading the morning paper that he'd only just had time to pick up, even though it was afternoon. He paused in his perusal to listen to the voice from next door and smiled.

Such a lovely woman.

15 THEN

There was only one place Wendy could go.

Bradley Woods wasn't as close as her home, in fact it was about twice as far away, so she couldn't run all the way there. She had to stop twice, each time starting again but slower. In the end, she couldn't continue. Her chest was burning and her legs were heavy. She felt her heart and mind were doing exactly the same. She had no choice but to walk.

Wendy's face was wet with tears, many of which had stained her shirt. She was sobbing. People stared at her as she passed them, but she didn't notice. All she could think about and all she could see was the look on Pagan's face as the girl's own boyfriend prepared to… And the sound of the cheers and jeers.

"Are you all right, love?"

The voice hung in the air and she left it behind. She barely heard it anyway, and wasn't interested in the concern of strangers. All she wanted was to get to the comfort of the trees. Her quiet place.

She thought someone else might have spoken to her but, again, ignored it. Then she felt arms on her.

"Wendy, are you OK?"

It was Brenda, the woman from the floor above hers. She was nice. A pleasant, rotund woman who always had a cigarette hanging from the corner of her mouth. It appeared stuck to the thick layer of dark red lipstick she always wore. The cigarette's end was actually an inch of ash that clung precariously to the tip. Apart from her recognition of the neighbour and the nature of the 'cancer stick,' as her mother often referred to it (while smoking herself), Wendy didn't hear what the woman was saying. The lips were moving and the eyes were wide and only half blinking, the lids seemingly unable to fully close because of the concern they were so full of.

Wendy stood, allowing herself to be gripped and shaken, as if her state was transferring into the other as agitation. She didn't fight it, not at first. She wasn't within herself. While her body was being held captive by Brenda, her mind had continued on to the Quiet Place. She'd mentally arrived there, so Brenda's interruption was happening somewhere else, to someone else.

"Come on," said Brenda finally, walking with Wendy following. "Let's get you home to your mum and dad, eh?"

Wendy abruptly snapped back into herself. The thought of her parents seeing her like that was enough to awaken her and she needed to escape her neighbour's grasp.

"Wait," she said, stopping. "I just need to wipe my eyes and blow my nose."

Brenda nodded, handing the girl a cloth handkerchief she pulled from her sleeve. Wendy took it and did as she'd indicated she would. Passing it back, it slipped from her fingers.

"Oh, I'm sorry!"

Brenda tutted and looked down. She bent to retrieve the square of now tainted material and, when she looked up, Wendy was gone.

The break forced on her by the neighbour had given Wendy's body the chance to recuperate some of its lost energy. She was running again. With her eyes and nose dried, she looked like just another girl, albeit one who had somewhere to be. This time, the distance was shorter and the breathless stops were absent.

She sat, more calmly than she might have done had Brenda not restrained her.

"What am I going to do, Wonder?" she asked the air.

Being a hamster, she didn't respond, but Wendy knew her friend was there and felt comforted because of it.

"I just…" she began.

"Who are you talking to?"

She spun around. She hadn't heard any leaves rustle or twigs snap, though her attention had been torn between the school and her pet. Who would dare…

Oh.

Samuel Thomson. Tomo. Terry's best friend, though he wasn't as much of an idiot or sycophant. Wendy quite liked him, but not in a liked him way. He just wasn't as bad as the others. He did fine at school, better on the few occasions he applied himself. He was clean, had never been seen picking his nose and eating the findings and he didn't always join in with the ridicule tossed around by his friends and other students at anyone they thought it might stick.

But, why was he here? She didn't think he was the sort to lose-himself-to-find-himself in a forest. Saying he wasn't as bad as the others didn't preclude him from the usual misbehaviour exhibited by almost all boys his age. And many of the girls, too. A trip to the Woods would, most likely, involve climbing trees. They'd be collecting conkers. Finding a stick long and firm enough to try and hit squirrels or pretend it was an extension of their penis.

The boys', not the squirrels'.

Wendy couldn't help herself. She smiled at the dirty joke her mind had made. Tomo, being the cocky and deluded boy he was, thought the smile had clearly been for him. She was pleased to see him, which was cool after what happened back at the school. She must like him.

Good.

"Tomo, what are you doing here?" Wendy asked.

She wanted to tell him to leave, but perhaps the company and comfort of a decent boy would help her recover. And, maybe, he'd put a good word in back at school. It was worth a try. She'd see just how nice he could be.

"I came to find you," the boy said. "I followed you to make sure you were OK after... all that back there."

"Yeah, but where's Terry> Where's all that gang you lot are so bothered about?"

"Pagan's a bitch," Tomo sneered. "Terry just wants a piece of the popular girl. He don't mean anything by it."

"He was going to..."

Wendy couldn't bring herself to say exactly what the boy was going to do. She felt a racking sob rise in her chest, but forced it back down, though she was less successful with the tears that crept from the corners of her eyes, hoping they'd go unnoticed.

"He's not here," Tomo said quietly.

He put his hand on Wendy's shoulder, ignoring her flinch. She didn't remove it, though. It felt nice. Comforting, along with the unexpected softness in his voice.

"Look, come back to school. I'll tell Pagan where to go and I'll protect you. Don't worry."

"You...? Why? Why would you do that?"

"I'm not like them, Wendy. You know that. I hate it when Pagan does stuff like that. No one stops her. Everyone laughs, but not 'cos they think it's funny, it's 'cos they're glad it's not being done to them."

Wendy nodded. He probably wasn't wrong. She'd always thought everyone liked Pagan. Actually, everyone wanted to be liked by her. Such was her influence, she had grown the reputation of being 'top girl' when, in fact, she'd only managed to propagate one of intimidation disguised as popularity.

"Are you OK?" he asked her.

She paused, but then nodded again. She was feeling better, thanks to him and the realisation Pagan's acceptance wasn't something she really wanted. She just wanted to not be an outcast. Have a friend. Maybe that would be Tomo.

She smiled.

"Wanna hug?" he asked, releasing her shoulder and putting his arms out to welcome her.

A third nod found Wendy moving closer to the boy and allowing herself to be enveloped in his arms. It was a purely platonic embrace, she felt. A friend wanting to comfort a friend. Tomo held her like that for a good minute, not moving, allowing her to be calmed and to relax. To feel safe. She didn't want to break away, so was disappointed when he moved.

He dropped an arm, keeping the other around her.

He scratched his leg.

He brought his hand back up but, this time, Wendy felt her skirt being lifted.

It took a second for her mind to catch up with what was happening. To realise everything Tomo had said was fake.

She tried to pull away, but the arm still around her stiffened to hold her in place. The embrace was deliberate. Planned. She put her hands on his chest and pushed. He resisted easily, his straying hand rejoining its sibling to restrain her further.

"Get off me, you shit!" she shouted.

Tomo started laughing. His face was close to Wendy's and she could feel droplets of spit sprinkling her face. She winced and shook her head in a futile attempt to rid herself of the liquid. He pulled her closer, leaning in for a kiss. She squirmed, but held too tight to avoid his lips on hers. When he brought his head back, he was grinning.

Wendy spat in his face, simultaneously bringing her knee up to his groin. The boy swore loudly, but released her. He fell back, groaning, his hands between his legs.

"You bitch!" he yelled. "I'll fucking kill you!"

It was Wendy's turn to laugh.

"I'd like to see you try with crushed balls, you bastard!"

She moved closer to him and brought her foot back to kick his stomach. As she swung it forward, he grabbed her ankle and pulled. It was Wendy's turn to stagger and fall and Tomo took the opportunity, the pain between his legs forgotten for a moment, to scramble on top of her.

"You're mine now, slag!"

"I'm nobody's! Get off me!"

"That's not what I'll say, slag. You're everyone's. That's what you told me. Anyone who wants a go can come and get a piece. That's why you're left your knickers at home. No one would be stupid enough to believe something Pagan told them, would they?"

"No," Wendy shouted, writhing beneath him. "She said I could…"

"Could have any boy you wanted if you showed 'em your bits. We all know. Slut."

"No! That's not true! You know…"

"I know you offered me some, but I didn't want a bitch whore like you. No idea how many've already been up there."

"No… no one has," Wendy whimpered, the fight leaving her rapidly.

"Course not," Tomo sneered. "Who'd want someone like you? Ugly bitch."

He slapped her and she screamed, a piercing sound that quickly deteriorated into sobs. How could this have happened? Why did shit like this keep happening? Tomo slapped her again, then again, his laughter becoming manic. He was enjoying himself.

Wendy's head was knocked from side to side with each hit. She'd closed her eyes against the impact and the pain, but opened them again, as she felt his hand go to her chest. She reached out, her hands grasping at anything that might help. She touched something solid and, not caring what it was, brought it up, hard against his head.

Tomo's temple made a crunching sound as the rock smashed against it.

16 NOW

Wendy yawned.

Sleep had evaded her the past few nights, something that had haunted her on occasion all through her life. At times, she was able to lay down, close her eyes and not opened them until morning. Sometimes, more recently, it would be late morning and she'd berate herself for wasting half of the day, particularly as she had guests downstairs in need of looking after. Other times, however, sleep danced at the edge of the room, right where the floor and wall met. It was darkest there in her bedroom, with the meagre light seeping in at the edges of her thick curtains not quite managing to reach that far. Wendy would tell herself, and other, she preferred it completely dark at night. Lamps had to be off and curtains or blinds drawn. She'd be restless otherwise.

She would never quite pull the curtains to the side to close the small gaps that allowed the subdued illumination from outside to sneak in. In fact, if her handling of the curtains meant those gaps disappeared anyway, she would make a show of straightening the cloth to neaten it. Not to make the gaps.

The darkness at the edge of her room would extend a hand towards the stray tendrils of luminescence, then snatch it back before the other could make contact.

Wendy imagined such things on the nights where, no matter how hard she tried to sleep, she still lay awake. Still thinking. Pondering. Remembering. She thought, or hoped, letting her mind wander to these fantastical ideas would find the rest that so eluded her.

It didn't, and had never, but it made sense to her. Don't focus on any one thing. Let your mind drift where it wanted. Don't push it and it would return the favour by allowing you to nod off.

Theories and facts were often enemies of one another, so she was regularly left staring at the ceiling at 'silly o'clock'.

Wendy found housework and entertaining were the best cures for the lethargy she so often couldn't shake off. They concentrated the mind and injected energy into her mood that would sustain her for hours. Still, however, she had her lapses. Still, she yawned, something entirely unlike the lady she saw herself to be. Still, she would find herself stirring a cup of tea and lose moments. Or an hour, though that had only happened on two occasions.

She yawned again. Perhaps it was time for a nap. She didn't usually try to sleep during the day as the light pushed against her closed eyelids, trying to force them open. Maybe this time would be different, though it was doubtful. Her guests would be fine for a little while.

Wendy didn't like to think she wasn't being the perfect hostess. She felt a pull towards the dining room that was difficult to resist. Did they want a biscuit? Another drink? The bathroom, though that was unlikely given their state. Lee, in particular, needed her attention. New guests received special treatment to ensure they had a long, pleasant stay.

But, just a little nap.

She started to walk to the stairs. As she passed the dining room, she couldn't help but open the door a sliver.

"I won't be long," she said to the occupants.

She took their silence to be a sign of acceptance, so closed the door and went up to her room. Though she would often awaken on her back, with the first thing she always did on opening her eyes being looking for faces and forms in the bumps and curves of the artex, Wendy went to sleep on her left side. The right hand side of the bed had always been hers, back when she shared her bed with her husband. Now she slept alone, that hadn't changed. In place of his body was one of the plump spare pillows that decorated the head of the bed. It gave a little weight to where he used to lay snoring and grunting, with her watching him, smiling warmly.

She closed her eyes, telling herself to remember more air freshener was needed for the dining room. She meant to get it when she went shopping, but it had slipped her mind.

And, for once, Wendy did sleep.

And dreamed.

Dreams are our subconscious' way of working through the problems our conscious minds have but struggle to deal with.

Apparently. Or they're a journey through our fears or our stresses. Perhaps it's the mind's way of pruning all the billions of pieces of information, recognised and unnoticed alike, to start the new day clear headed. A dream could even just be the way the mind keeps itself active to continue functioning properly.

Or, maybe, a dream is simply a random collection of nonsense images coalescing into a story, however haphazard that might be.

Wendy walked along a path in the woods. It was narrow, with tall trees lining each side, but she didn't feel claustrophobic. When she looked down at herself, the bushes filling the gaps between the trunks would brush against her arms. They were not trying to restrain her, they were just wanting a second of contact. Someone to notice they were there. When she looked up, the tree tops were thick with branches and foliage, creating a complete cover that blocked out any sunlight, but it wasn't dark. She could see easily and, again while looking up, she saw the trunks bent away from her, giving her the space to move without crowding.

Looking down at herself, Wendy was in her school uniform. She looked to be, and knew she was, sixteen. With her eyes diverted to view the surrounding forest, she was an adult. Still younger than her physical age, but much older than her sixteen year old self. And the transition was instant and transparent. There was nothing odd about it. She was three ages at once, and it was completely normal.

Dreams allow the abnormal, the extraordinary, to be entirely ordinary. Wendy would comment more than once in her life that she wished the real world was like that. You could do amazing or dastardly things, and it would be as if you have just switched the television on, Mundane.

The pathway extended too far in front for her to see the end. She just knew she had to get there. Something was waiting for her. Or She had to wait for something. Or something. It didn't matter, she just needed to find where the path terminated.

Walking was getting her nowhere. Literally, it seemed. The bushes looked the same. The trees were almost identical. If she hadn't seen the ground moving beneath her, and that it was repeating with every step, she would have believed she was on a treadmill like the one her father had bought, insisting he would use it. It did, of course, remain in its box until they moved house, and then it was sold with the proceeds being spent on cheap lager and cheaper cigarettes.

She started to jog, picking up a little speed in the hope there was actually a destination and she wasn't remaining in the same spot.

The bushes, who only wanted to say hello to this girl, took umbrage at her increased speed. This time, they did try to grab her. They did try to hold her in place. Only because they wanted to say hello, of course. There was no ill intent. They were only bushes, so had no such feelings.

As their twigs touched her arms and tried to wrap around them, she yanked away, snapping them easily. If one was too tight, she would twist and snap them off her. The bushes tried harder, using their leaves, overlayed upon each other for better tensile strength, to wrap the twigs. Still, Wendy succeeded in pulling herself free.

She was running now. As fast as a crying, humiliated girl had once done. She could feel her heart beating in her chest and, when she glanced at her shirt, she could see its outline, a perfect love heart shape, even though she knew this to be a romantic twist on the organ's true shape, throbbing against the material. Was it trying to break out? To get in front and win what was somehow becoming a race? She pushed herself harder. Her heart would just have to stay where it was. She wouldn't allow it to be freed, at least until she'd reached the end.

Further on, on either side, Wendy could see the smaller shrubs being picked up by the larger bushes, aided by the trees' lower branches. They were being absorbed, melting into the body of the bigger sibling to make a new, more massive creation.

Now, there were no more twigs. No more leaves. A mass of vines, woven intricately around thick yet supple branches reached into the space in front of her. They wove around each other, creating a wicker effect reminiscent to a basket she'd made in school. She was so proud of it, and had received a merit from the teacher. Her mother had used it as an ashtray and sworn at her when the hot ash scorched it.

"It's ugly now. Typical of you to make something that doesn't last. You won't last, girl. Mark my words. You won't last."

The basket had been thrown out, and Wendy felt as if part of her had been disposed of in the process.

She ducked forward, bracing herself, preparing to smash through the obstruction.

When she hit it, she could feel it break, hear wood crack and splinter.

But it held. The vines tying it together were not as easily damaged.

Wendy couldn't move, caught in a spider's web of verdure that refused to let her go.

She could feel something dripping down her cheek. It reached the corner of her mouth and she stuck her tongue out to taste it.

Blood. No doubt her own.

"What do you want?" she shouted.

The answer was a whisper on the wind as the vines moved from the branches to wrap around her. And tighten.

"A friend..."

17 THEN

Wendy dropped the rock and scrambled up.

She was shaking. Panting. Had she killed him? Was she a murderer? No! He attacked her! It was self defence, wasn't it? It had to be. She didn't mean to hurt him, not really. It was the heat of the moment. Instinct. She was just protecting herself.

Yes, that was it. They'd believe her.

"You bitch!"

She'd been staring right at the boy, but hadn't noticed him get up. Or stagger up. Tomo was on his feet, though unsteady. He was holding the side of his head and blood was seeping through his fingers. He blinked his eyes a couple of times, then looked up at her.

"You tried to kill me!"

"No! No, I didn't! You were attacking me! You were going to... going to…"

She couldn't finish the sentence. Her mind didn't want to go where he had been leading and she wasn't going to allow him to make her feel guilty for forcing her hand. What was she supposed to do? Let him?

"You kidding me? You think I'd wanna touch you? I'm gonna kill you and tell everyone what a slut you are. Beggin' for it and cried when I said no."

"You won't! You can't!"

Wendy's face was wet with tears of fear and anger. The former for what he might do to her, and the latter for both that and what he had already done. Her fists were clenched, but she didn't know if she had the strength, emotional or physical, to punch him. He could overpower her easily.

She saw Tomo clench his own fist and knew what was coming. She took a step back, not noticing the thick root waiting for her to trip against it. Falling back, she grabbed at the air to try and find something to stop her hitting the ground. A branch! It slowed, but didn't pause her momentum, instead snapping half way along its length.

Tomo ran at her. He was growling in a manic, animalistic tone that matched the mask his face had transformed into. One of fury.

He launched himself towards her, bringing his knee up as he moved. When he landed, that would either be forced into her stomach or somewhere much worse.

Wendy, sprawled on her back with nowhere to go, cried out and swung wildly with the branch.

It hit Tomo against the side of his head, right where the stone had first drawn blood. He grunted but still landed directly on top of her. Luckily for the girl, his knee made contact with the hard earth and she heard something break as it did so.

There was no cry of pain form her attacker, however. And no movement.

Slowly, she pushed him off, rolling him onto his back so she could get out and up. Still gripping onto the branch, she looked down at him. He wasn't moving. His eyes were closed. Was he…? No, he was still breathing. Wendy didn't know if she was pleased or disappointed to see the faint rise and fall of his chest.

She moved closer and pushed against him with her foot.

"Tomo?"

"Tomo? Sam?"

Another prod with the toe of her shoe. Still no response. One more go and then she'd leave him. He was breathing. He was alive. He'd be fine.

She reached out with her foot to nudge him but, as it touched against his side, Tomo suddenly reached over and grabbed her ankle.

"You're dea…"

Wendy's reaction was instant and instinctive. She was bringing down the branch on his head – his face, to be exact – before she realised she was beating him with it. By the fourth strike, Tomo had released her and was no longer moving. By the sixth, his face was unrecognisable, and he was no longer breathing.

By the ninth, Wendy was exhausted and stopped. The branch was bloody and broken, much like Samuel Thomson's skull. She let it slip from her fingers and absent mindedly wiped her hands on her skirt. She was feeling numb, as if all her anger and humiliation had been passed to Tomo through the branch. Looking up, Wendy saw, as if for the first time, they were in her quiet place.

It felt dirty now. Tomo being there and attacking her had tainted the calm atmosphere that had always pervaded the area. It was the unquiet place now. And, now, Tomo wouldn't leave either. Even if his body ended up being eaten by flies, maggots and foxes, he'd still be here. Not in the same ways as Wonder, of course. Wonder was welcome and her spirit seemed to remain. Tomo would be a bitter memory that would haunt Wendy more than his ghost could ever do.

She spat at him, the saliva splattering in what would have been his eye socket.

"Bastard."

She turned and started to walk away. She'd already missed the start of school. She'd be in trouble for that but, if she turned up, then she wouldn't be marked absent for the day. Maybe there'd be less of a punishment. She'd have to think of an excuse for not being there for morning registration and first period Chemistry.

To avoid bumping into Brenda, the neighbour, again, Wendy took a different route to school. She couldn't be doing with trying to explain why she was so upset earlier. Hopefully, the woman wouldn't bother to report it to her parents, but it was doubtful. While not exactly nosy or a gossip, Brenda liked to be involved.

She'd say something.

The new route took Wendy through a cemetery. It wasn't the main one in town and only really existed because the area had been its own village years before, until the town had grown enough to encompass it. Few new burials were carried out there anymore, though it was a popular place for the funeral service. Weddings too, but they didn't usually end up in the cemetery, at least not for a few years.

The calm shattered at her quiet place could be felt here, among the dead. They were silent, allowing her to pass undisturbed and work through her thoughts. Her thoughts, however, were as still as the bones beneath the ground. They had stalled, having no idea where to go next. She could, albeit mostly subconsciously, identify which direction to take, but any actual deliberation about actions was impossible.

Oh, if only she could stay there. The dead would understand her.

Her mind awoke.

Maybe she could! She'd live amongst the gravestones, with the spirits of the deceased to keep her company. They could tell her about their lives. Their loves. Their victories and defeats. And she could tell them about her... about her...

About her what?

What did she have to talk to anyone about? She was still too young to have really lived, and she doubted anyone, particularly dead people, would want to hear about her rocky relationship with her parents. They might be interested in listening to stories about Wonder, but that would take all of twenty minutes. What would she do for the rest of the time?

Perhaps the ghosts just needed someone to listen to them. They didn't need or want to do the same for someone still living. All that could be shared once she'd gone over to their side, whether that be upstairs or down.

Wendy knew she couldn't remain there. She'd be hungry. Ghosts didn't eat, nor did they need the toilet, she assumed (unless they pissed ectoplasm). Besides, she had to face what had happened. Tell her side, if anyone would believe her.

School it was.

She could have gone straight to a police station, but they wouldn't get it. Police were well known to be uncaring of children. They were after the wife beaters and robbers. Why would they take notice of the wild story from a school girl? At least, at school, the teachers were there to do just that. Listen to the children they looked after each and every day. Wendy would talk to one, and they'd make everything all right again.

She wasn't entirely convinced of that. Teachers had their favourites, and they had their own troubles. As impartial as they were meant to be, they were still people. They could still be swayed by the stresses Life would put in their way to trip them up or make them climb over. Hopefully, she could find one dealing with neither that could deal with her.

The cemetery needed to be left behind. As she made her way to the exit, she let her hand brush against the tops of the gravestones. There was an assortment of different types, from stone crosses and cherubs to the more common, classic vertical paving slab. Wendy preferred the crosses. Not for any particular religious reason, being unsure if she believed in a god or God. No, instead she liked them because they had a direction. Just like the arrows on a compass or map, they pointed towards the different ways she could go. With a cross, one in particular was longer than the others. Down. Yes, this was to help it be fixed into the ground and to stand proud, but it pointed down.

If you could always go down, it meant you were already up. No matter how bad you felt things were, there was always something worse.

18 THEN

The difference between being in the cemetery grounds and being beyond them, back in the 'real' world, was profound. Back amongst the dead, sounds were careful. They tiptoed around, remaining subdued. Leaves would be caressed by the breeze, allowing the noise to be a faint shift of greenery rather than a loud rustling. People spoke in hushed voices. Birds were reflective, pondering instead of singing.

In the street, no such care was taken. Sound left any reservations behind to escalate to noise. Cares, those previously reticent birds, children, life. They all jumbled together to crash against ones' ears in protest at being excluded from whatever lay though the tall, wrought iron, black gates.

Wendy winced against the sudden onslaught, but it was immediately forgotten. Being more used to the cacophony than its absence, the clamour could become white noise instantly. She felt enveloped by it and, though she'd welcomed the silence, the return of the commotion was met with gratitude.

The route she was taking back to the school was longer than the one she'd left it on. It was almost lunchtime by the time she saw the large building that served as both sports hall and auditorium. It was adjacent to the main school, but had a gap of less than a metre between the two. There was an adjoining door, encompassed by a the shortest of corridors, joining them, but otherwise the gap ran the full length of both.

By the end of break, there'd be a host of newly extinguished tab ends. Teachers knew the area was used by those students who smoked, even though it was against the rules and most were underaged. They ignored it for the most part, only doing random checks to oust the culprits when the weather was fine or they'd had a nice lunch in the, admittedly above average, school canteen. When they did catch pupils in the act, warnings were issued, but none carried out. What was the point when it wouldn't stop? Reprimands or detentions would always fail to deter children from smoking. They would do it anyway and, if not there, elsewhere. At least they were still on school grounds, so attending their lessons. It was an unhealthy, but necessary, compromise.

Once she was at the school gates, she paused. Should she have gone home first? Put on the underwear she'd so foolishly left behind? No. Her parents would have been home and returning to school was the better option by far. Still. Beneath her clothes she was naked. Up until that point, apart from when Tomo had tried to assault her, she'd forgotten about it. She was amazed she could, but it had happened. The severity of it had been undermined by that stupid, now dead, boy and the ordeal she'd faced with Pagan and her followers.

Now she was re-entering the very place her humiliation had taken place. She was nervous, but not as much as expected. After all, this wasn't the first time she had been shamed. It was becoming part of the school day. One day, she could see it being added to the curriculum. Between History and Geography, there'd be a half hour slot for the public degradation of her. There'd even be a test and Wendy knew who'd get top marks.

"Wendy?"

She looked around at the sound of her name, but couldn't immediately see who had spoken. Then she did. It was Miss Henry, one of the Physical Education teachers. Miss Henry was pleasant enough, so at least Wendy hadn't been discovered by someone like Mr. Reynolds. He was a tyrant in the class. No one could speak out of turn and he would take great pleasure in having a late comer or non-homework completer stand at the front of the class and read notes the man would hand over. They would be the lesson plan in snippets and the chosen child would be forced to read them and fill in the blanks, with shouts, jibes and detentions raining down if they got it wrong.

Miss Henry was barely taller than Wendy and it was the brick wall that the school gates were fastened to that had concealed her presence. The woman had clearly been running, something she was well known to do. Between lessons and after lunch, she could be seen jogging around the perimeter wall. She could easily manage half a dozen full round trips each day.

"Miss Henry," Wendy said, suddenly fully aware of her clothing predicament.

"What are you doing out of school? You're very late. I thought I saw you earlier, though."

"You did Miss," Wendy said quietly, not making eye contact in case the teacher could see her lack of underwear and the self defence killing she'd done in her expression.

"So…?"

"So, Miss?"

"So, where have you been? Why aren't you in class?"

"I…"

Her voice faltered and she had to clear her throat. No! She would not cry! She was the victim here!

"Wendy? What's wrong?"

Thinking she was holding back all signs of her torment, Wendy shook her head, but it was followed by her entire body trembling too. Tears started to flow and she wiped them away with the back of her hand.

"Nothing Miss."

"Don't give me that," Miss Henry said. "Look at you. You're a mess."

"S… Sorry Miss."

"Don't apologise. Just tell me what happened."

So, Wendy did.

Her words were a torrent that gave the teacher no time to interject with either words of comfort or shock. She included the incident at the swimming pool and the molestation in the school toilets. She spoke about the lack of underwear, but left what happened with Tomo out.

She only wanted to be liked. To fit in. She wanted friends, that was all. Why couldn't she have friends? Was she such an awful girl? She wasn't nasty. Wasn't a bitch. She tried to be nice. She really did.

"I try to be nice, Miss."

Miss Henry didn't say anything. She had no idea what words could fit the situation. The poor girl had been the brunt of the worst possible offences the teacher had experienced while being a teacher. Or ever, for that matter. She'd heard about the occurrences, but hadn't realised they were related. As horrified as she'd been about it, she hadn't delved any more deeply. Her own problems were more important. Her boyfriend's illness and the treatment that made him so much worse. Her rising debts. The fact that, though she really didn't have a drinking problem, she knew she might have a drinking problem.

She knew Pagan well and couldn't understand the girl's popularity. A bully shouldn't prosper so well. All the girls seemed to want to be her, and the boys wanted to be with her. And she knew it. And played on it.

Once, she'd found Pagan smoking in The Gap. She was with her gaggle of 'friends,' or those who said they were her friends to avoid being victims. It didn't always work. Pagan liked to make an example of random members of her gang by picking on whichever aspect of their appearance or personality she decided to be a target. It didn't put any of them off, though. It was never to the extent of the things Wendy had endured.

Pagan hadn't been named. It was obvious, however. She was the only one who would do such a thing.

"It's Pagan, isn't it?"

"It's.. No. Not her. It doesn't matter who it was."

"You don't need to lie to me, Wendy. It's quite clear."

Wendy shook her head. She didn't want to give any names. What was the point? It wouldn't change things. It couldn't take back anything that happened that day. Besides, it could lead to more questions, so prompting more information.

"Well, whatever you say," Miss Henry said, shaking her own head. "We both know what really happened."

They did? They knew what really happened? What, everything??

Get a grip, Wendy told herself. She means with Pagan, not the rest!

"Come on," the teacher said, putting her arm around the girl. "Let's go see the Principal."

Wendy resisted the pull from Miss Henry towards the school, but knew she had no choice. Why else was she there in the first place? After a moment, which the teacher gave her, she allowed herself to be led. Of course, it had to be lunch time. Children were pouring into the corridors and all, seemingly, knew about her. Instead of streaming towards the dining hall, with each child caught up in the combined current of all the rest, they stopped. They stared. They whispered. Some dared to laugh, but stopped after a sharp, direct stare from Miss Henry.

Wendy was taken past them all. She didn't make eye contact with any of her spectators, instead looking no higher than waist height. It was enough to see where she needed to go without seeing their faces.

The principal's office was on the far side of the school, and usually took an age to get to. She was surprised when they arrived at the door much sooner than expected.

Miss Henry knocked.

19 THEN

Principal Oftensted was a tall, robust woman with a feast of red hair that refused to be tamed. She'd been in charge of the school for long enough that none of the students had ever known anyone different. Many of the staff were in the same boat. Whilst some schools had a high turnover of staff depending on who was in charge and the relationships between them, Principal Oftensted only lost faculty members through maternity, retirement or, in one case, death. Teachers respected her and students feared her. It was a combination the woman liked and allowed to endure.

"Genny," she said, addressing Miss Henry. "What can I do for…"

Mrs. Oftensted had always made a habit of speaking to the teacher first whenever one turned up at her office with a child in tow. It wasn't often for anything good, so she felt the child should be made to wait. To feel secondary. To stew.

She would take a deliberately fleeting glance at the students involved. It helped emphasise how disinterested she was in them until the point she needed to be otherwise. One look at Wendy told her she needed to be interested.

"Come in, both of you! What on Earth is going on?"

Once the door closed behind them and Wendy was seated next to Miss Henry, the world outside fell away. The imposing sight of the principal and the comforting presence of the teacher made her feel finally safe. She was untouchable in that room. Was it time to tell all?

No. She couldn't. Not everything.

It wouldn't take long for Tomo to be reported missing. If nothing was said during the remainder of the day, and he was thought of as truanting – given those he associated with, it wouldn't be unheard of – then his parents would notice. Their son wouldn't come home.

Ever again. Terry would be questioned and it would come out about what happened that morning. Terry would know where his friend had gone. He'd no doubt tell the police, though he wouldn't give the information easily. It would implicate him in Pagan's game. In the end, he'd give up the information. Tomo would be found. Wendy would be arrested and charged, her version of events being diminished by the fact she hadn't come forward herself.

If she wasn't guilty of anything, why would she not tell someone straight away?

She had to speak up. As formidable as Principal Oftensted was, she could be trusted. Miss Henry too. Wendy knew they'd help her. They'd believe her.

Wouldn't they?

"Speak to me, Wendy," the principal said.

Her voice was kind. Calm. Enticing, even. Many a child had been caught by its tone and fooled into opening their mouths to let the words pour out. Wendy wasn't so easily caught out but, on this occasion, her defences were down. She opened her own mouth, but nothing came.

She stared at the desk, following the wood's grain to distract her while she tried to calm her thoughts. It didn't work.

"Come on," said Miss Henry. She took hold of the girl's hand and squeezed it gently. "You know you can tell us anything."

Wendy nodded silently. She knew, but she also knew exactly how it sounded. She'd been foolish, tricked by someone she knew was likely to do so. She'd led the boys on, one in particular. They'd fought. She'd hit him. Killed him. Then, she'd gone back to school to continue with her lessons as if nothing had happened. How much of a cold bitch did that make her?

"So…?"

Principal Oftensted leaned forward expectantly, with her elbows on her desk and her chin in the upturned palms of her hands. She didn't push the girl. There'd obviously been some sort of trauma, more so than had already happened to her. The poor child was holding back something new.

"I… Nothing, Miss."

"Nothing? Are you sure?"

"I'm OK."

"Well, if that's the case, perhaps we should just call your parents. You don't look like you should be in school today. Maybe you're under the weather. They can take you home and we can try again tomorrow."

"No!"

Wendy had been slumped in her chair up to that point, but sat up straight at the thought of her parents being involved.

"Is there a problem?"

Wendy was flustered. Yes, there was a huge problem, and she didn't mean them. But they would only add to the issues.

"I…"

She couldn't. She couldn't.

She had to.

"I killed Samuel Thomson."

20 NOW

Some people can still feel, or more likely act, as if they're still asleep when they awaken. A shot of caffeine can ping their minds back to full working form in an instant but, for the period up until then, they are more zombie than person.

Others are awake and aware instantly when the alarm goes off. Sleep is discarded as quickly as a bank balance on Black Friday. They can leap out of bed, ready to battle the world with refuelled vigour, leaping tall buildings in a single bound. Or, at least, taking steps a couple at a time.

Wendy was in the latter's camp, though her vigour would only refuel to a fraction of its once youthful exuberance. She didn't need an alarm, waking at 6:30am every morning, give or take a few minutes, since she was in her late thirties.

After this rare afternoon siesta, she was disorientated, but her mind was devoid of the fog that affected so many others. For a second, she forgot it wasn't early morning. Why was she dressed already? Why was the sun in the wrong…?

Oh, silly girl. She'd had a nap, that was all. Checking the alarm clock on her bedside table, which was only ever used for its time aspect, she sat up abruptly. She hadn't meant to sleep for so long.

Poor Lee would need settling in. She didn't want him to be the odd one out. She climbed off her bed and went down to the dining room.

"How are we all?" she asked everyone. "Are you getting to know our new friend?"

She paused, giving them the chance to answer, which they didn't.

"Excellent. Right, well, I just need to borrow him for a little while. Talk amongst yourselves."

She pulled some coiled tubes from behind the sofa Lee was

sitting on. Unravelling them, she attached one end to some apparatus tucked away in a corner. The other, she laid on the floor while she connected long needles to it.

"Oops," she said, giggling. "I forgot my peepee!"

By 'peepee,' she meant PPE, personal protective equipment, which Arthur wore religiously when working. She could never quite get the hang of the double P and thought it hilarious to say peepee. Arthur started to use the term himself, which made Wendy smile every time.

It must be because she'd just woken up. That was why it slipped her mind. She didn't want to get any mess on her clothes. That would be… not evidence… just… unfortunate. She had sheeting to lay out, which protected the furniture and carpet nicely, but her clothes were more personal. A splatter on the floor was an inconvenience. One on her dress would be like a mark on her soul. A blemish that no amount of bleach could remove.

"I'll be right back."

She hurried to the tall cupboard in the utility room. It housed her ironing board and vacuum cleaner and was also home to the lightweight polythene sheet she used, inherited from her husband. To him, it was the Blanket. Oh, he was a quirky one! Wendy noticed the Blanket was becoming worn. She'd have to rectify that. She already knew it could do with being replaced, but it somehow connected her to dear Arthur. She didn't want to give that up, so would continue to use it until it fell apart.

Back in the dining room, she ignored Lee's dead eyes looking so impatient. She was doing her best and he should realise that. She wasn't as sprightly as in her youth, but she still managed all the heavy lifting and cleaning on her own. Didn't he realise that?

No, don't get irate with him. She could see why he was tiring of waiting. He could probably feel the decomposition of his body and wanted her to work her magic to eliminate it. While she couldn't quite stop the process, she could delay it. When it had progressed too far, but not quite to the point of Wonder's maggots, she would have to send the guest on their way. It would make room for someone else, anyway. A fresh face. A new friend.

It was amazing how easy she found discarding a body. The cutting up. The sawing. The bagging and getting rid. She was numb to it now, so carried the task out as if she were simply washing the pots after dinner. It was something she didn't like to do, but it needed doing. So, she did it.

She laid the Blanket out neatly then pulled a gown from the bag of new disposables that was hidden along with the tubes. She paused, wondering whether she should take off her apron – how silly of her to sleep with it on – or leave it. It'd be double protection but, as with her clothes, it was more personal. Arthur had bought it for her for one of the last birthdays they'd spent together. He'd tried to resist, not wanting an apron to be a gift, but she had insisted. She needed a new one, so why not? He should spend his money on something she wanted and needed rather than something he thought she'd like. Ever grateful for everything she was given, especially from her husband, she would have accepted any gift and been happy, but at least this way, he'd be getting pleasure out of the apron too. All the apple crumbles and steak pies she baked with it on showed him how right she was.

Wendy took off her apron and laid it across the legs of one of her other guests.

"Hold on to that for a little while, would you James? I'll be as fast as I can."

James did as he was asked, not moving his legs so as not to dislodge the apron. He was a nice chap who had been delivering pizza takeaway menus. He was just about to put one through her letterbox as she'd opened her door.

He never left, though Wendy thought he had just about outstayed his welcome.

Working quickly, even with the arthritis in her fingers doing its best to slow her down, she inserted the needles in the relevant places. She barely had to look nowadays, so the dusky light through the drawn curtains failed to deter her. It was something she'd tried long before meeting Arthur and perfected since.

Draining a body's fluids and replacing them.

21 THEN

A breath drawn in a silent room.

In through the nose and out through the mouth. That's how she was taught by her mother to remain calm. Count to ten, or whichever number you needed, and breath in through your nose, out through your mouth.

Count.

Principal Oftensted was trying extremely hard to follow her mother's advice from so many years before. The woman was dead now, but she'd had so many wonderful little snippets for her daughter to take with her through life. As a child, Oftensted could be quick tempered. She would fail to listen to others, including her parents. While her father, kind though strict, would reprimand her, her mother would take the time to speak. They'd have a conversation. She'd pacify. Advise. The adult Oftensted continued her mother's legacy in becoming a teacher, then principal, in order to transfer the skills and knowledge she'd gained onto further generations.

Focus was one such skill. Keeping calm was another.

Principal Oftensted suddenly felt not as adept as she'd believed.

Miss Henry's face probably reflected her own, she thought. Never in her years had she heard such a barrage of vile abuse, culminating in the death of a poor boy. She didn't blame the girl, not really. She'd been provoked. Pushed to breaking point. But, still, she had killed Samuel.

Oftensted knew of young Mr. Thomson by the reputations of those he associated with, and now regretted that. She should know every child in her care. Ultimately, they were her responsibility, though her staff were the ones who fielded any immediate concerns. Perhaps, now, that wasn't the best course.

Focussed, she turned to Miss Henry.

"Genny, would you mind getting a glass of water for this young lady?"

Miss Henry nodded, taking the hint to leave the office. Usually, two adults were meant to be present when interviewing a child, but this was an extraordinary situation. She would get the water, taking her time to do so. By the time she returned, her boss would have the girl's attention and her trust.

"Now, Wendy," said Oftensted as she interlinked her fingers and rested her forearms on the desk. "Isn't this just a big bag of worms?"

Wendy thought it was much more than a bag of worms. She knew the principal was trying to play things down. It would be better for the interactions between them. It's not so bad, it's only murder. Come on, tell me everything and then you can go back to class and we'll say no more about it.

Except, it was bad. As bad as it possibly could be. She had nowhere to go, though. No one else to talk to. Most kids would run to their parents for the support a parent should give. Wendy would always choose to run away. Support, for them, was a beer mat from the local pub used to stop the kitchen table wobbling.

"Yes Miss," she said, not lifting her head.

"You know, you're going to have to tell me what happened. You do know that, don't you?"

Wendy knew. She couldn't blurt out 'I killed Samuel Thomson' without repercussions. Miss Henry had passed her on to the principal, probably because she didn't know what else to do. If they hadn't met at the school gates, Oftensted would have been her destination anyway. She'd done the worst part. Getting there and making the initial statement.

OK. Right. Wendy took a deep breath, then let it out, hoping it would take with it a whole dollop of her fear. Surprisingly, to a certain extent, it did. She gripped the arms of her chair and leaned forward.

She expected the story to take much longer than it did. So much seemed to have happened in the woods but, going through it, there really wasn't. Tomo had tried to trick her into believing he was being nice. When his true colours were revealed, she defended herself. She played down the ferocity with which she hit him with the branch, thinking it would make her sound less than totally innocent. Why carry on smashing in his head once he'd been stopped?

Because… well, because she needed to make sure he wasn't going to get back up again. Not because it felt… no. It didn't feel good. It didn't. She didn't get caught up in the sensation of bones shattering. She…

Principal Oftensted was speaking and Wendy hadn't been listening.

"Pardon?"

Oftensted stopped mid flow, took a breath and began again. Often, she would be angry at being interrupted by a child or a student. She expected to be listened to. Notice taken and words acted upon. She could understand why Wendy might not be concentrating, so would allow the infraction.

"You've been through a terrible ordeal, Wendy dear. I can't imagine what it must have felt like. I certainly can't imagine the same thing happening to me. Being assaulted, threatened, right on top of what Pagan had done – and don't worry, she won't get away with her part. Now, I need to call the police. I need to think about how to tell the school. And I need to call his parents."

Wendy's face dropped at the mention of the police. She'd hoped they could be left out, but wasn't naïve enough to think that would actually happen. They had to be, really. Someone had died. She'd killed them.

She nodded.

"And, of course, I'll call your parents. I'm sure you want to see your mum."

Frantically, Wendy shook her head.

"No, Miss!"

"No? What, you don't want your parents called?"

"No, Miss. Please."

"Why not?"

That was a question she didn't know how to answer. She couldn't tell the truth, if it would be believed. Parents didn't act like hers did. Or shouldn't. The last thing she wanted was them there. They'd feign concern. Pretend love. Then, when they were back home…

"Just… please don't."

"Unfortunately, we don't have a choice, my dear. It's school policy, for a start. Besides, I'm sure you want them here really."

"I really don't, Miss."

"Wendy, listen. The police will need to speak to you. I don't think they'll arrest you, but they will interview you. Investigate and so on.

95

You need your parents for that. You can't face it on your own. You'll need their support."

Wendy didn't answer. What was the point? It didn't matter how much she protested, Principal Oftensted was adamant her mother and father were there. She knew it had to happen, whether she liked it or not. She might as well concede.

"OK, Miss," she said sullenly.

It took thirty minutes for the police to arrive and another fifteen for her parents.

"I'm sure they're busy," Oftensted apologised to the officers when they arrived. "They'll be here soon."

When they finally did enter the office, Carol and Eddie were a whirlwind. He came in with an arrogant swagger in his step, as if daring the police to pin any of this mess on him. She followed closely, her eyes searching the room for her daughter and turning dark when she saw her.

"What's all this shit?" her father said gruffly.

He squared up to the officer closest to him, PC Evans, but the other man didn't flinch. Instead, he stood straighter, which brought him a good six inches taller and as many broader.

"I'm afraid yo…" Oftensted began.

"I'm not talking to you. I'm asking this cop here."

The principal shrank back a little, not used to being put down so abruptly and not knowing exactly how to deal with it. She didn't respond, allowing the policeman to take the lead.

"Your daughter here is in something of a situation, sir."

"A situation? You're saying she's killed a boy. That's more than a 'situation'! Anyway, are you mad? She's too much of a muppet to do anything like that. Likes playing with dead animals, but that's about how far it goes."

"That's as may be, sir," the officer said. "But it seems something very serious has happened and we need to look into it."

The second officer stepped forward. Unlike the first, she was neither tall nor broad, but her tone when she spoke showed neither was required to be noticed.

"She likes to play with dead animals?"

Eddie laughed and Wendy winced. Why did he have to bring that up? It made her look like a death loving maniac. And laugh? Didn't he see how he looked to the police?

"Is something funny?" PC Atkins asked, raising an eyebrow.

"You do realise the severity of the situation?"

Her emphasis of the last word made Wendy's father frown. Was she ridiculing him? She'd better not be!

"Well, it's a joke, innit? This poor streak of piss couldn't kill anything. Her hamster needed a hand, or foot, from me. She kept the little rat after it'd snuffed it. Got all maggoty and stunk. As if we didn't know."

"Is this true Miss Whipnale?"

Wendy nodded slowly. When it was explained like that, it sounded ludicrous. Who keeps dead animals? You throw them away or flush them down the toilet. You don't make them a bed and keep talking to them.

Except, Wonder was much more than that. Wonder was a connection to someone or something else. Someone other than her own thoughts and reflection. That's why she clung on to her for so long. And still did, spiritually.

"She was my friend," she said quietly. "I didn't want to lose her."

"She was dead, you stupid little..."

"Sir!" PC Atkins said, raising her voice and abruptly cutting off the man. "Sit down and be quiet!"

Eddie didn't argue. He was too surprised. The grin had gone and he did as he was told. Carol took his place.

"Don't you speak to my Eddie like that! Who do you think..."

PC Evans clapped his hands loudly. Everyone froze and stared at him.

"Let's calm down here, shall we?" It was a statement rather than a question. "We're dealing with a possible murder here. Mr. And Mrs. Whipnale. It's good to see you obviously care for your daughter, but we need to proceed with our questions, if you don't mind."

There were no further comments, so he sat next to Wendy and leaned forward.

"Could you tell us what happened, please?"

22 THEN

Even though you know every detail of a story to tell, sometimes, the mind can forget some of the specifics. The colour of a person's eyes. Whether or not they were wearing a coat. Gender and age. It's the bane of a police officer's life when they're trying to piece together evidence, particularly from multiple witnesses. From one, it can be just as bad. Multiple retellings have a habit of causing those very same details to change. It's not deliberate, and the person in question being questioned doesn't realise the differences.

Wendy's story was identical to, though not necessarily word for word (which could sound rehearsed), as she'd told Principal Oftensted and Miss Henry. Later, PC Evans would ask the teachers if they could corroborate what the girl had said, and they did. There were minor changes, but not in anything important.

Evans believed her. He hadn't attended that many murder or suicide cases, but had children of his own. He'd been around criminals too and recognised signs of lying from both. Wendy was telling the truth. She'd killed a boy, but he felt for her. He'd help her.

It was a sure bet her parents wouldn't.

It was a difficult time for the officers, the teachers and Wendy herself. It was impossible to keep what happened at the school that morning secret, so there didn't need to be much digging to find the culprits. At first, they all denied it, then tried to say Wendy had instigated it all. That was before Thomas, Pagan's ex-boyfriend, came forward and told what he knew. He covered everything, from the swimming pool to the toilets to Pagan's plot. He told how Wendy was always the odd one out. She was different. Not strange, but not entirely normal. She tried too hard to fit in and that made her even more of an outsider.

Terry was the first to break. Being told that he was part of the reason his friend had died snapped his already weak resolve. The promises Pagan had made to him, what she'd allow him to do if he kept his mouth shut and what she'd do if he didn't, paled against the risk of being implicated. Being a suspect himself. He could go to prison. Be expelled. He'd be in the newspapers, and he knew shit stuck. He wouldn't be able to shake off the stigma, ever.

So, he told his own story. How Pagan controlled most of the kids in the school by fear or by assurances of popularity and success. How he couldn't help himself when she told him to touch Wendy. It was difficult to refuse Pagan, let alone go against his hormones. It wasn't his fault!

Except, it was, he was told. If he said no or defended Wendy, his friend might still be alive. He wouldn't be being interviewed by the police.

Terry was crying by the end. Evans and Atkins ignored his tears, being used to bullies themselves. Although neither had been victims, either at school or generally in life, they'd had friends who had, and dealt with other children who'd suffered. His tears were real, in contrast to those Pagan produced when she was questioned, but he was still complicit.

In the end, no charges were brought against Wendy. She acted completely in self defence and her continued beating of Tomo was excused because of the intense stress she was under at the time.

"I had to make sure he wasn't going to attack me again," she'd said. "I didn't want to die."

Pagan, of course, was expelled, along with Terry and a number of the others who were part of their group. They blamed Wendy, as they would. They'd just been 'messing'. She should know how to take a joke. Samuel Thomson's family blamed her too, but moved away soon after their son's death and divorced not long after that. It was a separation long overdue, but Tomo's passing made it easier for them to realise their relationship wasn't working.

Eddie's car was egged. The paintwork was ruined thanks to the keys used to scratch swear words into the doors and bonnet. The tyres were slashed. Excrement was pushed through their letterbox and smeared over the door handle.

"Why not just give him what he wanted?" her mother had asked one day. "It's part of life, stupid girl. You didn't have to kill him for it."

They had no choice but to move, the new location being an actual house rather than a flat. Wendy's room was larger and they had a garden. She liked it and so did her parents, though they never told her that. It was always her fault they'd had to give up their beloved home. Her fault she had to be put into a new school. Her fault money was tighter. Her fault she was such a burden.

Wendy became even more introverted but didn't mind being alone anymore. Friends couldn't be trusted, so she wouldn't have any. At least she wasn't shunned at the school. She wasn't treated as a target either. She was, in the most part, ignored. For her, that was just how she liked it.

Well, she didn't like it because, no matter how much she told herself otherwise, a real friend was still…

No. Friends couldn't be trusted, so she would push anyone who tried to get close to her away. Not that anyone wanted to. For the first few weeks, she was just another newcomer who no one really cared about. They had their own gangs and cliches already. She clearly didn't fit into any of them, so why bother?

Apart from the ongoing demands of her parents, Wendy finally felt relaxed. She began to smile, something she hadn't done for too long. Her parental abuse didn't abate, but nor did it increase. Had killing Tomo given her some courage? Some confidence?

It was a shame his body had been taken away. She would have liked to have gone to the service, a cremation, but her father had laughed at her when it was suggested.

"I'm sure his mum would give a big welcome to the girl who battered her son's brains in with half a tree!"

She didn't go.

His body, however, would have been something. She would have called him Samuel. Treated him with some respect. Maybe, eventually, he would have forgiven her for the damage she inflicted on his skull and his mortality and she, in turn, could have forgiven him for what he had planned to do.

She could have introduced Samuel to Wonder, and the hamster would have been able to keep him company for the times she couldn't be there.

A month and a half into her time at the new school, Wendy bumped, literally, into Lisa.

Tall and skinny, with dark eyes surrounded by almost as dark circles, the girl with long hair a similar colour was staring at the floor as she walked. The were in the hallway going from class to class and someone had muttered something as they walked past Wendy. Her legacy had yet to follow her, so it was unlikely the other child was speaking directly to or about her, but Wendy couldn't help but glance back to make sure. The pair collided. A bag was dropped, books were strewn and apologies were made. And the girls carried on their way.

Three days later, they were passing each other again, though both were looking in the directions they were meant to. The girl's gaze was still cast downwards, but she noticed Wendy and smiled. The smile was hesitant and wary, but there. Wendy smiled back. Hers was equally as cautious. She wasn't used to others being pleasant to her so was unsure how to react. A couple of hours later, at lunch, they found themselves next to each other in the line into the cafeteria.

"You're watching where you're going now," the girl said quietly.

A boy in front of them looked back and frowned. His eyes moved up and down the girl and his expression changed to something resembling a shrug. He wasn't impressed. His attention returned to how slowly the queue was moving.

Wendy nodded but didn't say anything. She was waiting for the punchline. Or the punch. Neither materialised.

"I'm Lisa," the girl said. "I don't... talk much to anyone."

"Wendy. How come you're talking to me?"

"Because nor do you. I figured you know what it's like."

"What what's like?"

"To," her voice dropped to a whisper. "Not fit in."

Wendy stared. Was it that obvious? She'd tried to be relaxed. Confident. She knew her attempts weren't fully successful, but were they that bad?"

"I need to go," she said. "Toilet."

She left the line and hurried away. Her stomach growled its frustration at being so close to being filled, but it wasn't the first time she'd gone hungry. It would quieten down soon enough. In the meantime, she went to the library. There were few in there at the best of times, so lunch time was bound to be quiet.

It was. Apart from Mr. Hampshire, the librarian and one of the best English teachers in the school, there was only another girl present. Mr. Hampshire looked up and smiled briefly before going back to the book he was reading. The other girl was engrossed and appeared to not even notice someone had entered the room. Wendy went to a table as removed from them as she could manage and pulled a book out of her school bag. She'd been reading it sporadically, but not been fully committed to the story. Now, as she needed something to distract her and focus her mind on the trials someone else was going through, she decided to change that.

Head down, resting on the knuckles of a loose fist, she soon lost herself in the story.

"Did I do something wrong?"

Wendy looked up, startled. The girl she'd escaped from was standing in front of her. Her hands were intertwined, but the fingers refused to remain still. Wendy recognised nerves when she saw them. She'd suffered from them enough over the years.

But, why be nervous of her? She was a nobody who didn't want to be a somebody.

"Huh?"

The girl (Lisa wasn't it?) indicated back towards the door, clearly meaning the cafeteria.

"Did I offend you?"

"Offend me? No, why?"

Wendy was becoming agitated quickly. She didn't need a spotlight on her. That brought unwanted attention. She wished to remain in the shadows, being overlooked by everyone.

"You ran off. I only said 'hi' and told you my name. Then, you were gone. I didn't know if I'd upset you or something."

"Would it matter if you did?" Wendy asked. "Not that I'm saying you actually did or anything."

"It would, to be honest."

Wendy hadn't expected that. For her entire life, no one had cared whether she was upset or offended. Her mood had never been questioned. Or considered. What game was this girl playing?

"Well, you didn't and I'm not. But I am reading."

Lisa sat down at the table, positioning herself opposite Wendy. The latter stared at her book, pretending to read but taking nothing in. Leave me alone! When the other girl failed to do so, Wendy sighed and closed the novel.

"What do you want?" she said. She tried to not sound irritated but couldn't hide it entirely.

"My parents keep telling me to make new friends. I've never been good at it before, but know I have to try. They say being alone all the time isn't good for my social skills, or something like that. Figured, if I made the effort, it would get them off my back."

"So you're speaking to me just to get back at your parents?"

Typical, Wendy thought. Just use me.

Lisa shook her head.

"No. I'm not saying they're right, but they might not be wrong."

"So, why pick on me?"

"I'm not trying to," Lisa said. "I'm just trying to make a friend."

"Like I said, why me?"

"'Cos you're on your own like me. I've seen you around school. You barely talk to anyone. Never look up. Don't interact with no one."

"I'm interacting with you."

"That's only because I sat down and gave you no choice."

"I do have a choice," Wendy pointed out. "I can ignore you. Maybe walk away."

"But, you're not."

Wendy thought about her options. The girl was weird, but that was maybe a good thing. It meant they had something in common. For whatever reason, this Lisa wanted to be her friend. What if…?

No. She'd seen how that ended up. She wasn't going to go back there.

She closed her book and put it back into her bag, then stood. She looked at Lisa, wondering what, if anything, to say. Nothing was probably the best option, so she walked away in silence.

"I'm just trying to…"

Wendy turned suddenly, ripping the end off the girl's sentence.

"Leave me alone," she said, turning before the tear threatening to fall on her cheek could be seen.

23 THEN

Wendy couldn't decide if her parents were feeling sorry for her or playing a cruel joke.

She entered her room one day after returning home from school. Her routine was to change out of her school clothes, usually into her comfiest pair of pyjamas, then complete any homework she had to do. She'd then eat, making her own food and anything her parents wanted. They were fed up, they said, of Wendy wasting good food. They were tired of running around after her. They weren't her slaves!

So, she became theirs, in a way. Making her parents' drinks extended to sorting their breakfasts which expanded to making the evening meal. Plus washing pots and clothes. Vacuuming and ironing.

They were making her self-sufficient, she was told. Making her more attractive, because she was on to a loser if she wanted to rely on her looks.

She entered her room, in the process of pulling the scrunchie from her hair. She didn't see it immediately, but heard it. A slight squeak from a wheel in motion. A slight squeak from the rodent running on it.

Another hamster.

She squealed in delight and ran to her bed, cradling the cage in her arms, her eyes filling with tears. After catching her breath, she ran down to the living room. Her parents were sitting on the sofa, arms folded, waiting for her.

"You saw it then?" Eddie asked, smirking.

It wasn't the smile of a loving parent wanting to hear how wonderful their child thought they were for the huge surprise they'd just discovered. It was condescending, a look he'd perfected. Usually, it would have stopped Wendy in her tracks. She'd be wary. Fearful.

She was too excited, though. She saw the smile and misinterpreted it as that of the father of another child. Her mother looked expectant but disinterested. She was probably missing a television programme for this. Again, Wendy saw something else entirely. Expectant, yes, but of the welcomed forthcoming embrace. The effusive thanks.

"I did! Thank you!"

"Yeah, well you better look after this one."

"I will! Of course I will! She's adorable!"

"She's a he," Carol said. "Try not to get this one killed."

Wendy grinned and nodded, the fact she wasn't to blame for Wonder's death not occurring to her.

"And no maggots, either," Eddie added. "We don't want none of that stink, got it?"

"Got it."

"In fact, just keep it out of our sight."

Unable to contain herself, she threw herself at her father, wrapping her arms around him tightly. His own arms remained by his side, not returning the embrace. If Wendy noticed, she didn't care. She moved to her mother to repeat the gesture, but Carol stepped back and put her hands up.

"None of that nonsense, thanks. Just go make me a cuppa. And I'm hungry."

Wendy nodded. She would have done anything for her parents at that moment. Mugs of hot beverages made, she started cooking dinner. Desperate as she was to return to her bedroom, she knew she shouldn't. Not until food had been served, eaten and pots washed. Then the evening would be hers and she could introduce herself to her new friend.

The weekend was three days away, and it dragged. Wendy spent every possible minute with Curious, whose name was derived from her favourite book, Alice in Wonderland. The hamster enjoyed being held and would sit in her hands for extended periods while she stroked it and spoke softly about her days, which seemed to have improved immensely. The weekend, however, was going to be special. She would have the whole day with him. Two days, no less.

And she had plans. She'd ensure he never left her.

Weekends brought with them chores she couldn't do during the week. The laundry and ironing were two, but anything else her parents thought of could be added. Wendy was up at the same time she woke on a school day, and had everything completed by the time she would have left. She heard her parents talking in their room, so knocked and took in drinks and toast.

"Can I go out now?" she asked excitedly.

"Where to? Where are you rushing off so early?"

"I just want to take Curious out for a bit. I want to show him around."

"Curious?" laughed Eddie. "Where do you get these stupid names from?"

"From Al…"

"I don't care. You do know it's a hamster, right?"

Wendy nodded. She knew exactly what Curious was, and he didn't have a stupid name.

"He's not a dog. You can't just stick a lead on and walk him down the street."

"I know, but I just want…"

"Go," her mother interrupted. "Just don't come back for a bit."

Carol looked at her husband with an odd smile and moved closer to him. Eddie mirrored the smile and nodded.

"Yeah," he said. "Take all the time you want."

At most other times, Wendy would have noticed the look between her parents and understood its meaning. She would have balked at the thought of her parents' sexual activity. Thankfully, she was blinded by her eagerness to show Curious the world. She went into the kitchen then, placing the hamster gently in her coat pocket, left the house and started walking. She couldn't help smiling and that, plus her constant chatter as she told her pet about everything they were seeing, prompted questioning stares.

She ignored them all. She was fully aware of each one, but didn't care. The streets were filled with topics of conversation, no matter how mundane, so why not talk about them? Curious sat calmly in her pocket and listened intently.

Well, that's what friends did, wasn't it?

Another reason Wendy liked where she lived was because of its proximity to the woods. Bradley Woods and its equally woody neighbour Dixon's were just outside of town. A road led between the two, continuing on through a stream of villages until it reached Waltham, a small town that clung to the term with pride, even though it was barely more than the villages preceding it. On its far side, Waltham spread out to merge with the edge of her home town, the two bonding seamlessly across a busy road. Bradley and Dixon's, established well over a hundred years before, were much closer to her home than her old one. Escape was that much easier.

Bradley Woods was the one most people went to. It had a small car park, full of potholes from lack of maintenance. A play area consisting of a couple of swings and a piece of rope over a mud filled dip and the remains of a slide was situated in the centre and a narrow path surrounded the whole forest, splitting it in two half way around to create a pair of semi-semi circles. Smaller paths led off the main one, spidering through the trees, but they were only partially cleared from infrequent footfall. They could only really be called 'paths' because they gave a sense of direction. The illusion of passable gaps.

Dixon's was much more dense, so much less visited. There were no discernible paths leading in any direction through it. The trees stood tall and close, with bushes surrounding their bases like bowing worshippers. Any clearings were purely accidental and were just waiting for the forest to notice then fill them.

If the previously mentioned road wasn't there, the two wooded areas would very likely become one. As it was, the A16 kept them apart, allowing them only to view each other across the tarmacked surface, never to meet or touch. Never to combine. Never to attain completion.

It was Dixon's Woods that Wendy decided to go to on this occasion. Wonder was in Bradley, and she didn't want her old friend to be jealous of her new playmate. Curious wasn't a replacement. He was an addition. She would ensure her father's foot never came into contact with him.

She'd only ever ventured inside on one previous occasion. Usually, she didn't even notice the place was there. Bradley was always her intended destination and thus her focus. On this occasion, she would discover its secrets along with her pet.

Turning left at the entrance, she climbed over the wide metal gate. It had a heavy padlock fastening it closed, one she would have expected to be rusty from the elements but that was, in fact, looking well maintained.

"Here we go," she said quietly.

She stepped beyond the threshold of the tree line. It was an odd feeling she knew was more psychological than reality, but she couldn't help the sensation of being enveloped by the mass of the forest. It wrapped its metaphorical branches around her protectively.

"Feel that?" she whispered to Curious. "It wants us here."

She walked on, taking care to watch where she was going. The thick undergrowth hid myriad hazards, such as roots and dips and thorns, any of which could trip or scratch her. Rather than try to discern a 'proper' direction, she wandered aimlessly. Birds sang of her presence, celebrating her arrival. She listened and smiled. Of course, they weren't actually tweeting about her and the forest hadn't taken her in, but in her imagination, that's exactly what was happening. She was, she told herself, entitled to her fantasies.

Wendy passed through the occasional clearings without stopping. She wanted one, but not just any. The Goldilocks one. Not too big, not too small. Not too dark, but not too light. Eventually, after feeling as if she must be reaching the other side, she found one that was just right.

It was kidney shaped, with one not quite circle overlapping another, slightly smaller one. A bald patch of ground gave the curved back of the kidney. A thick branch had fallen from one of the surrounding trees and gave the chance for her to sit. The branch creaked under her weight, but held.

"OK, Curious. We're here."

She took the animal from her pocket and held him on the palm of her hand. Lifting it up to eye level, she smiled at him.

"We've found a new quiet place," she said softly. "Isn't that nice?"

Curious nuzzled her skin in agreement.

"Now then. I've got some treats for you."

24 THEN

If she were a hamster, Wendy thought, she would be happy.

A hamster is fed regularly. It's cleaned out, has a wheel for exercise and fun and no responsibilities. And it is loved.

Curious was definitely loved. She'd brought him some special treats that would show just how much. They'd prove she'd never let him go.

Carefully, she placed him on the ground. He sat, sniffing around, but didn't move.

"Go on," she told him, patting his bottom. "Have a little wander."

Curious scurried about, exploring the area. She watched him and smiled again. He really did make her happy. What did the world look like from a hamster's point of view? Was everything huge, making you feel tiny and insignificant? Wendy knew how that felt. She could sympathise.

From the pocket Curious wasn't sitting in, she brought out a flattened cardboard box. Pushing it back into shape, she placed it on the floor near her beloved pet. Next, she picked up some leaves and laid them in the box as bedding.

"All you need now is a nice lamp."

She laughed and Curious looked up at her, his little nose twitching.

"I know, you prefer standing lamps. It's OK, you can decorate it however you like."

She lifted him up and put him inside his new home, then stroked his back.

"We'll be together forever."

Wendy sighed, a contented sound that showed she had everything she could ever need. Why couldn't all life be like this?

Why couldn't everyone be nice like she was? Like Curious was? There'd be no reason for tears or being afraid or hurt.

She pulled out a small container and shook it. Not many left.

Gloves. Best use gloves. She couldn't wash her hands out there and didn't want to risk putting her fingers in her mouth. Luckily, she came prepared.

Once the gloves were on, she opened the container and emptied some small pellets into her hand. Having no idea how many would be required, she filled her palm. Better to safe. Better to make sure.

She leaned over.

"Look what I've got for you, Curious!"

Carefully, Wendy tipped her hand so the pellets poured into the corner of the box. Once done, she moved the few stray ones closer to the pile. Finally, she laid some of Curious' food on top.

"Now, I don't expect you to eat it all in one go," she said. "You take your time. You'll never leave me now, and I'll always be here for you. Best friends for life, OK?"

She removed the gloves, turning them inside out as she did so, and gave her friend a last stroke of his back.

"I have to go," she said. "I'll be back tomorrow, I promise."

As she placed the lid on top of the box, she saw Curious sniffing at the pile of rat poison.

Good. Eat as much as you like. I'm sure it's really tasty.

She left the kidney gap, as she thought of it, behind and made her way back through Dixon's Woods to the road. Once there, she paused, deciding which way to go. Her parents had wanted some alone time, and that was one thing she did not want to interrupt. She'd go left. It was a long walk, but that was fine. If she was still out, away from home and her parents, she was, in a way, with Curious. Their connection wasn't broken.

There was a bin by the side of the road. It was in dire need of emptying, the disposed of picnic remnants and general refuse poking out through the access holes like demons escaping the gates of Hell. Though it felt gross, she moved some of the rubbish aside so she could push in the gloves. She kept the poison in her pocket. Her father would notice its absence so it would need returning.

She gave a mental wave to Wonder as she set off. It would have been nice to go and see her, but Curious was the girl's priority at that moment. Wonder would understand.

There was no path next to the road. It was too 'country' and not enough people used it for pedestrian access. The rare houses along its length, until the next village, were either farms, a large elderly care home, or homes for rich people. One was a lottery winner who thought his newfound millions gave him the right to be arrogant and treat people in such a way he became widely disliked. Wendy had heard her parents talking about him, partially jealous because of his wealth (they never won anything, they said, even though they never entered anything) and partially to gloat that his money was supposedly running out. Such places were primarily visited by car, so there was little need for a pathway. Wendy didn't mind. There was enough of a grass verge to keep her off the road, and she was aware enough to walk into oncoming traffic rather than with the flow.

When she arrived home, her parents were still in their bedroom. She could hear her father snoring and her mother whispering. Was she talking to herself? On the phone? Either way, it meant they were occupied, so Wendy had a little respite from their spite. She made herself something to eat, washed and put away her plate and glass and went to her room.

There, she laid on the bed. She stared at the ceiling and smiled. She now had two friends. Both hamsters rather than other children, but that was fine. Friends were friends. Neither would leave her and she could easily spend time with both. Just not at once.

She slept. It was a deep, contented slumber that gave her dreams she didn't remember on waking.

After school the next day, and each day, she went back to the forest. Her father had taken to going to the pub for a drink around the same time each day and her mother was either lost in the television or out on her own. It meant Wendy had no issues with visiting Curious before going home and, occasionally, even Wonder.

She could tell the poison was having an effect on her pet and, rather than worrying about any discomfort he might be in, she was thankful. The pain would be short lived, then he'd never suffer again. And never leave her.

It did occur to Wendy that Curious would soon be in the same situation as Wonder. They'd both be dead. Both rotting or rotted. Both gone from this world and onto any that may exist after. The difference was, her father had murdered Wonder. Crushed her and enjoyed doing so. Wendy, on the other hand, was easing Curious into death. It was a loving gesture that would mean neither of them would ever be alone again.

On the fifth day, Curious didn't move. The poison had taken effect. The job was done.

Wendy lifted the animal out of the box and held it for a long time. She stroked him behind his ears and along his back. She spoke to him. Sang to him. Sat in silence enjoying the peace with him.

With regret, she realised she needed to go, so prepared the box for the next stages. Vickes, rubbed along the top edge of the lid, would disguise Curious' growing odour. Fresh bedding would make sure he was comfortable, particularly with the fact he'd no longerbe defecating on it.

The hamster's corpse lasted longer than Wonder's, decomposing at a slightly slower rate. Wendy found this fascinating. She'd expected them both, being the same species, to take the same amount of time. It was a good thing she'd discovered it so early on in her life. Who knew when the knowledge would be useful. The maggots came. More friends, she thought. She didn't spend as much time with them, though. They weren't exactly welcome, but were just doing maggoty things. She couldn't blame them for being true to themselves. It was something she intended on doing herself.

One day.

After a week or so, of course, the maggots became flies and left. Well, friends couldn't be counted on, could they? Except you, at least, Wonder and Curious. The flies were just using the latter's carcass for a feast. Their friendship was false and Wendy knew this. She'd called them friends but treated them as acquaintances. Someone she used to know but wasn't close to. Not like her hamsters.

Their departure didn't leave a hole in Wendy's whole. She could have shrugged her shoulders if she'd felt the need to. Her pets completed her, so she was happy.

25 THEN

When Wendy was a child, divorce was a dirty secret no one spoke about. Marriage was for life, whatever sort of life that might be. Couples took their wedding vows seriously, or at least those they wanted to. Adultery still happened. Cherishing sometimes didn't. Many couples stayed together because they loved each other. Others stayed together just because. Because it was the done thing. Because it was easier than facing the world alone. Because of the children. Because divorce was expensive. When she was an adult, when she was now, divorce was much more commonplace. She'd been to one wedding of a friend where they'd ran a sweepstake on how long it would last. The groom had bet two years. He'd been correct.

Wendy's mother, then, had already split from her father, a man who had never seen his daughter since, and Eddie had taken his place. Her step father, though she had never called him that and, if she had, he'd not have taken it well, had remained with his wife not because he loved her, but because he didn't dislike her. Though he'd never admit it, even to himself, Eddie was aware he wasn't exactly a prize catch. He changed jobs almost as often as he changed his underwear. When he was between employment, he had no qualms about making false benefit claims. His fists would often have their say before his brain had pushed the words down to his mouth.

Carol accepted that in him because she saw similar traits in herself. She had a man by her side and in her bed. Not much of one, but one nonetheless. She wasn't the best cook, but he wasn't a fussy eater. She didn't bother with her appearance too much, but the television didn't judge and Eddie wasn't bothered. She was accommodating when she needed to be, but could hold her own against his moods when the occasion demanded.

They suited each other, until they didn't.

Their breakup did not take as long as some. There are those who are breaking up almost as soon as they've declared their love for one another. Cracks begin to show but are papered over with false apologies or under breath swearing. With Eddie and Carol, their decline happened in a matter of a few weeks. Arguments, which had always been commonplace, escalated. Their time out of the house, individually, increased. Wendy heard her mother in the lounge on more than one occasion. She was crying.

Then, once day when Wendy returned home, there was only her mother.

She'd been drinking and was unconscious on the sofa. On the floor next to her were empty lager cans and an almost empty bottle of vodka. Wendy tried to rouse her, but was greeted by a slurred stream of abuse before Carol passed out once more.

Wendy went into the kitchen. She'd cook for herself. Make a drink. Relax. Think.

So, why was she standing at the sink with the cupboard beneath it open? Why was she staring at the rat poison?

Her parents couldn't decide who would have their daughter. Eddie, to his credit, didn't tell Carol her daughter was nothing to do with him. They weren't blood, so he had no responsibility. He refrained from turning his back on her. That didn't mean, however, that he volunteered to have the girl. More arguments ensued. Carol tried to insist she couldn't afford to bring up a daughter on her own. Eddie said they should share custody, but Carol should take the majority of the share. He told her, in earshot of Wendy, less booze and smoking would mean more money was available for food. Wendy knew each of her parents drank and smoked in equal amounts and couldn't see either of them reducing their intake. Carol told him where to go, except in far more expletive terms.

In the end, they shared her. Alternate weeks at alternate houses. Generally, life remained the same with either parent. She lived there, but neither house felt like a home. At her father's, she had to cook all meals, something spared her at her mother's. Carol lived on takeaways. Only one or two meals a week were made in house (by Wendy), with every other night being pizza or kebab or burger. Eddie didn't eat takeaways. He preferred what he called 'real' food. He also didn't comment, and Wendy didn't ask, about the takeaway wrappers he'd occasionally forget to throw out from the weeks he didn't have her.

Sleeping arrangements did differ. At Carol's, Wendy still had her room. At Eddie's, there were two bedrooms. One was his and the other had a padlock on the door. Wendy never discovered what was inside. She didn't ask and he didn't offer the information, other than to simply tell her never to touch the door or even think about trying to get inside. He'd know, he told her. She'd regret it.

He gave her two options for sleeping. She could sleep in his bed, a king sized one with sheets she was sure hadn't been washed for far too long. He usually slept naked, he said, but would make the exception and sleep in his boxer shorts. That was as far as he'd go, though. Clothes in bed made him uncomfortable. She didn't want him to be uncomfortable, did she?

Her other option was the sofa. It was large and filled with cushions and, in contrast to her father's feelings when clothed while sleeping, was surprisingly comfortable. For Wendy, it was the easy option. The only issue was, Eddie went to sleep when he felt like it, whether his daughter was tired or not. Sometimes, he'd still be awake after midnight. He'd be watching a film and not be concerned that she was falling asleep on the chair and had school the next day. If she lived in his house, she followed his rules.

It could have been a difficult time, but Wendy put the issues aside, locking them away in a vault she created at the back of her mind. It was an enormous room lined with endless shelves. Recessed lights hidden in the ceiling illuminated everything, banishing any shadows that might try to sneak around. In the floor, channels were carved allowing the clearest of waters to run through, filling the vault with the sounds of the ocean.

The vault's door was twice as thick as her arm and constructed of solid metal. It swung silently on massive hinges and, once closed, had an automatic lock that could only be activated by Wendy's special word. As she had yet to think what that word might be, she was safe in the knowledge the thoughts and memories she put in there were safely hidden away.

Eddie lived too far from the woods for her to walk when she wanted to visit either Curious or Wonder. She had to wait, at first, before she could get back to them. Her mother wouldn't allow her out, despite her objections, and she needed to take a bus from her father's, followed by a fairly long walk. A distinct lack of money and time prevented that. After a few weeks, however, her mother was habitually asleep when she returned home from school, an empty vodka or whiskey bottle by her side. When this was happening every day, Wendy took her chance to not go straight home.

The entrances to both woods were opposite each other, so Wendy was torn as to which friend she should visit first. Her only option was to flip a coin. Heads, curiosity for Curious won. Excitedly, she hurried through the forest, which was thicker than the last time she was there. The summer months had been kind to the bushes, given them the incentive and sustenance to grow. It meant the way through was tougher, the twigs scratching her legs and the branches obstructing her. She enjoyed it all the more, though. Maybe Curious had planned it that way so she had time to prepare herself for Wendy's arrival.

Finally, she did arrive and joyously lifted the lid to her hamster's home.

"What's that?"

.

26 THEN

Wendy froze, with all her body's potential movement being diverted to her heart, making it beat so fast and so hard she thought her chest might explode.

She knew the voice but couldn't place it. It didn't belong here, that was for sure. Young. Female. Who else would come to the woods?

Well, they were meant for the public, so anyone could. The thought hadn't really occurred to her previously, and its sudden appearance shocked her. Anyone could find Curious. Anyone could take him! Her friend would be stolen and alone and Wendy would be devastated. Curious hadn't taken the place of Wonder, with both friends taking up equal amounts of space in her feelings, but that didn't diminish how much she'd be upset. It was different with Wonder. Her first hamster's body was gone. There was nothing to find, so Wonder was safe. Curious was still there in physical form and this posed dangers she hadn't considered.

And now, they'd been discovered.

She put the lid back on Curious' home and carefully pulled some leaves closer to try and obscure the view of the box. Slowly, she turned around.

Lisa?

"What are you doing here?"

Wendy's heart had suddenly calmed and her shock and, yes she admitted it to herself, fear had turned to indignation. What was this girl's deal? Hadn't Wendy made it clear to her she wasn't welcome? Wendy didn't do friends, except those she chose, and that amounted to Wonder and Curious. They were ample. Besides, Lisa had clearly followed her there. That was just… weird!

Lisa didn't answer immediately. She scuffed the leaves with her toe, revealing the dried mud beneath. Her toeing continued into the earth. Perhaps Wendy's obvious anger made her want to bury herself.

Well, get on with it.

No. Don't. Not here. You weren't sharing space with Curious. You weren't taking him away from me!

"Did you follow me?"

Lisa nodded, still not saying anything. Wendy had been followed before. She should have been more careful! Was Lisa going to attack her?

"What do you want?"

Lisa's mouth opened and closed with no words being offered. She just kept fidgeting with her toe digging into the ground.

"Well, get lost. I don't want you here."

"What are you doing here?" Lisa asked, finally leaving the mud alone. "What's in that box?"

"Nothing," Wendy snapped. "Get lost, weirdo."

"I'm not a weirdo."

"You're not a weirdo, but you follow people into woods and sneak up on them?"

"I didn't sneak up on you. I shouted you ages ago, but you ignored me. You can't blame me for that."

"But you still followed me."

"I might have been here already. I could say you were following me."

"Yeah, but we both know I wasn't."

"I guess."

"So..?"

Wendy was fast becoming impatient. She didn't like to be surprised, and the other girl wouldn't be able to convince her it wasn't weird to follow someone. She needed to get rid of her somehow.

"So, maybe you're right, but it wasn't in the creepy way you're on about. I did shout you. I just couldn't catch you up."

"OK, if you say so. So what do you want?"

"I just wondered what you were doing, is all."

"Why?"

"'Cos... Well, just 'cos."

"You can't say 'just 'cos' and reckon that makes it all fine."

"Well, I already said. I'm supposed to make friends, but I'm shit at it."

"But why me?" Wendy asked. "I told you I'm not interested."

"Yeah, you did."

"So, why are you even here then?"

"'Cos I know what happened to you before. Maybe you could do with one yourself."

Wendy felt cold inside. She'd hoped the terrible experience was fully behind her. Why wasn't it?

Still, if she rose to the news, it would bring it all back to the surface, then drag her back down with it.

"I don't need anyone. I've got my own friends here."

She immediately regretted her words. Hopefully, Lisa wouldn't notice it. She wouldn't wonder what here meant. Unfortunately…

"Here? Who else is here? You're on your own, aren't you?"

Well… yes and no, Wendy thought.

"I didn't mean right here. I just meant… like… around."

Lisa nodded slowly, but tried to look behind Wendy to see what she was hiding.

"What's that?"

"Nothing!" Wendy knew she was a little too emphatic then. She needed to remain calm. Not raise suspicion. "Look, just fuck off."

"Tell me what that is and I will."

Wendy didn't move. She didn't want to show anyone Curious. The hamster belonged to her. No one else. Besides, no one else would understand.

"Nothing. It's nothing."

"So, show me."

"It's nothing. I already said."

"If it's nothing, you've nothing to hide," said Lisa. "Besides, if you don't show me, there's nothing to stop me waiting for you to go then coming to have a look myself."

Shit! Wendy couldn't take Curious home, to either one. Neither parent would accept the presence of an animal that was, it would seem, dead. Like Lisa and everyone else, they wouldn't understand. They wouldn't try to.

Fine! If it meant getting rid of her, Wendy could show her Curious' home. It'd freak Lisa out anyway, and maybe scare her off. Maybe then she'd not be a bother again.

But what if she told everyone at school? She'd be a laughing stock again.

"I can't," said Wendy.

"Why not?"

"You'll tell everyone. They won't get it."

"I won't tell anyone. No one even notices I'm there half the time."

"Yeah, but you'd do it just to get in with them."

"Did doing what Pagan said get you in with them?"

Wendy shuddered at her old bully's name. She hadn't heard it for such a long time, and hoped she wouldn't need to again. A fist clenched inside her chest, taking it's time to release. She shook her head.

"Exactly. Besides, I'll show you something."

"What?"

"You first. Show me what's in that box, and I'll show you something."

"No way. I'm not falling for that."

Lisa thought for a moment, then nodded to herself.

"OK," she said, taking a deep breath. "I'll show you."

Lisa took a step forward and unbuttoned the cuff of her sleeve. She paused and looked at Wendy.

"You won't say anything will you?"

Wendy shook her head. She had no idea what might cause such a reaction in someone. Lisa seemed to be fighting with herself. Arguing. She was clearly torn. In Wendy's case, she didn't want to share her pets, but also knew what other people could think. Would think. She didn't know much about Lisa, but didn't think there'd be anything that could be as profound as her own secret.

"Promise?"

"Yes."

"Say it!"

"Yes, I promise I won't say anything."

Wendy was keen to avoid any spotlights. She would prefer to divert attention away from herself rather than inviting it in. If she did tell anyone about whatever Lisa was going to reveal – and who would she tell anything? – it would ensure she was as involved as the other girl. Her silence, therefore, was partly to protect Lisa's secret, but also to protect her own anonymity.

With another deep breath, Lisa pulled up her sleeve.

At first, Wendy didn't know what she was supposed to be looking at. An arm? So what? What was so special about… Wait… What's that...?

Running along the back of Lisa's forearm were a series of extremely thin and light parallel lines. Scars. Wendy frowned. What could make marks like that? She'd not seen anything like them before.

"What are they?" she asked. "What happened?"

"What are...? Haven't you seen them before?"

"No. What are they? Have you had an accident or something?"

"No," said Lisa. "It's not an accident. It was deliberate."

"Did someone at school do it? Not your parents, was it?"

Wendy's experience of parents hadn't included much in the way of violence, at least not directly aimed at her (poor Wonder), but it made her acutely aware that it was a possibility. Perhaps not from her mother, but certainly from her father.

"My parents? No, not at all. They'd never... No, my parents are great. Aren't yours?"

Wendy decided not to comment. She didn't want a discussion about the different approaches to parenthood because that would be divulging far too much information to someone she barely knew. Whatever Lisa was showing her was obviously something major to the girl, but Wendy wasn't sure she could go that far herself.

That didn't mean Curious wasn't important, it just meant Wendy wanted to keep her private life private. No one needed to know Carol and Eddie weren't a perfectly loving mother and father. She hadn't even told anyone, including the school administration, she had two addresses. As far as anyone was concerned, they all lived in the same house and were happy.

"So, what is it?" she said, ignoring Lisa's question.

"They're cut marks."

"How did you get them?"

"I did them myself."

27 NOW

Embalming always left Wendy exhausted.

She was well used to carrying out the gruesome task, though she was numb to its grisly side, but she found it emotionally draining. Welcoming a new guest into her home was one thing. Preparing them so they were able to join in with the group was another.

She wanted them to get on with each other. Bond. She believed everyone had a side to them they wanted to hide. Whether that be secrets or self-disgust, people just were not completely honest. She, herself, had kept things from almost everyone in her life. Loved and loathed ones. Her dining room, filled with complete strangers to one another, was an opportunity for those secrets to be either laid bare or forgiven. For friendships to be made.

It was a gift she was giving. It was part of herself that she was giving.

During the embalming process, Wendy spoke to her new guests. She told them about herself, details only those in the room knew. She trusted them to not share any of those particulars with anyone else, which she appreciated. Sharing was part of their… initiation. She didn't expect them to do the same for her, of course. To the newcomer, she was just an old woman who was being nice. They knew nothing of the caring, generous person she was.

She realised it was difficult for them too. Being introduced into such a select group of individuals could be daunting. She wanted it to be a smooth transition, which was partly the reason for her sharing. Generally, they settled in well and stayed for an extended time. At least until they started to smell.

Personal hygiene amongst the dead wasn't a priority.

Leslie, a lovely woman who'd been searching for her lost dog in the park along with her daughter Vienna, was beginning to smell,

Wendy had noticed. She'd liked Leslie. They been getting on so well, especially during her time in the dining room. Vienna was a joy too. She was in her mid-teens and wore far too little clothing for both her age and the weather, but you couldn't tell kids these days, could you? It wouldn't matter so much now she was dead, Wendy supposed. Apart from her attire, Vienna (what an odd but sweet name) was never any trouble. Her manners belied her youth and she was always so animated. The girl was constantly talking and full of a life the deceased often lacked.

If Leslie had to go, and Wendy was sure she did, Vienna would leave too. Like mother like daughter. Wendy would be sorry to see them go, but there was only so much space in the room. Her house wasn't overly large, with the rooms being a decent size though not unmanageable. If new guests arrived, existing ones had to depart. The ones who'd been there the longest were often the ones whose decay was more advanced. Wendy was an amateur embalmer, something she'd admit herself, though not necessarily to herself. Her work worked, except not quite as well someone's with better equipment and more experience would. The coat of varnish she always applied to block pores and make their skin simply shine helped act like a form of glue for the flesh, but it, too, wasn't a miracle cure.

Time gave Wendy the chance to keep her friends around for longer than was often the case and she was grateful for that. Time, however, had things to do. A natural order to sustain. Wendy couldn't expect her friends to be completely untouched. Just that touching to slow.

Once the embalming of Lee was finished, she moved him into place. He'd asked to be seated between Leslie and Agnetha. Or Anegtha. Or Agethna, maybe. The woman's accent had been thick, coating her quite good English with an equally thick layer of treacle that glazed the inner ears and prevented the full understanding of her words. Wendy hadn't properly caught the correct pronunciation of her name. It was fine, however. Angegthgna answered happily to Aggie now she was dead.

With Leslie leaving soon, there'd be plenty of room for the newcomer. Perhaps Wendy would invite someone younger in to fill the space that would remain. They'd not take up so much room, so it would be a little less crowded. No one had yet complained about things being cramped, but Wendy didn't want to give them any reason to not be completely satisfied with their treatment whilst with her.

She'd never have believed caring for the dead could be so demanding. She'd also not alter a thing. She had her friends and her place in the world. Why would she want to change that?

When Lee was seated properly, Wendy gave him a cushion behind his head.

"You must be tired," she said. "Relax for a bit. Maybe you could get some sleep. The others won't disturb you, will you?"

She glanced around the room. No one argued, as Wendy expected. She smiled. They were such a lovely group.

"I'll be back soon with some tea and a little supper."

She opened the door to step out into the hall. Something didn't feel quite right. There was a tug at the back of her mind that refused to step forward and be seen. What was it?

"Come on," she said. "Show your pretty little self."

It remained just out of consciousness' sight, a shadow in the shadows of her mind. She waited patiently to see if it would slip up and reveal itself, not really expecting it to. It was becoming more common to have these snippets being snipped away and running free. She couldn't always pin point what memory or thought had become dislodged, either. She'd lived a long, full life, so there were a lot of both for her to lose, but she would have preferred to keep a hold of them for a while longer.

The best way to remember something, she knew, was to stop thinking about it. If you pushed, it would just become more stubborn and deliberately keep out of reach. If, instead, you were to focus on something else, something mundane, it would try to sneak back up to the forefront of your mind, inching its toe into view, ready to snatch it back if you looked its way. You could wait, still pretending to concentrate on the else, and complacency would seep in. The toe would extend to an ankle to a leg to a GOTCHA!

Wendy sighed. Even though she knew her thoughts needed to be diverted, it was difficult to not be concerned about her mental deterioration. It was a sign that her time on Earth was waning. Her body couldn't keep up with what she needed from it. Hadn't it been well looked after for all these years? She'd never been a smoker. A rare drinker. Junk, or fast as it was commonly called, food was something she avoided. She didn't feel she'd missed out on anything. Smoking and drinking weren't things she'd felt the desire to partake in, so why didn't her body repay her kindness with a few less years of infirmity? Why did it have to fail so soon?

She had too much work still to do. New guests to welcome. Old guests to dispose of. She wasn't ready!

Unfortunately, no one wanted to listen to her. Time had its own agenda, and she was an insignificant blip in its plan. All her friends had followed her dear Arthur over to the other side, so she didn't have them to speak to.

Wendy was certain of her uncertainty when it came to an after-life. It depended on what day it was and whether she'd had her first cup of tea that morning. It depended on whether her dress was green or blue. Whether her hair fell just right when she brushed it, or if it became sentient in the night and wanted to do exactly what she didn't want it to. While she didn't have issue with faith in things unproven, she did prefer to see or hear or touch. Otherwise, one couldn't be sure it was real. A girl called Pagan, way back when she was young, had instilled a mistrust of promises. The years had shown Wendy that some were kept. They'd also demonstrated some were not.

It gave her a tendency to be somewhat changeable in her choices. She wasn't one to hesitate, she just went with her feelings at the time. Given the same options, she would potentially make different decisions on different occasions. Each one would be right in that moment.

When she was dealing with her guests, she believed. It was more for them than her, though it was sincere. She was taking their lives and giving them eternity. When thinking about her own mortality, her view was not as defined. She didn't wonder about Heaven or Hell. In her mind, if there was anything, it would just be one place. Vast and unlimited. You'd continue there eternally, along with everyone else who had ever walked the Earth. There were no angels or demons, there was only simple serenity, the trials of humanity and Life left behind.

If there was nothing, you would cease to exist. No darkness. No Limbo. Just nothing. As you'd be dead, you wouldn't know. Life was life and death was the end of it.

Closing the door to the dining room, Wendy went into the lounge. She stood in front of the large window and stared out at the park opposite her house. It was a position she took most days, losing herself in the dog walkers, the children playing, the lovers and friends. She had been there for approximately thirty minutes, her mind diverted as she'd wished, when she suddenly realised what the tug was.

She'd forgotten something. Something important. Something she'd never forgotten before and needed to deal with immediately.

As the thought occurred to her, the something made itself known.

Lee's mobile phone rang.

28 THEN

Wendy had heard of self harming, but had yet to be exposed to its effects or know anyone who hurt themselves in such a way. When Lisa showed the marks along her arms, Wendy didn't put the name and the act together immediately, even when the other girl told her they were self inflicted.

"Why would you do that?" she asked.

"Why do you breathe?"

"What?" Wendy frowned, confused.

"Why do you breathe? It's a simple question. More than yours is."

"Because I have to. I'd die if I didn't."

"You would, yes," Lisa said, looking at her arm and running her fingertips over the scars.

"So, what's that got to do with that? I don't understand why you'd do it to yourself? Doesn't it hurt?"

"It does, or it did when I did it."

"So… I don't understand."

Lisa looked up to Wendy, thinking of the best way to say things. It wasn't easy to put it into words. Talking about it at all wasn't something she'd expected to have to do. She only showed Wendy to create a bond. There wasn't meant to be a discussion.

"My life is great, right?"

Wendy nodded, smothering the twinge of jealousy with a deep breath."

"I'm still an outsider, though. I'm happy, but I still find it hard to make friends. I feel too different and everyone's meant to be the same. But I'm not."

Wendy could empathise. It was just how she felt herself. Perhaps the two of them could be friends after all.

"But why hurt yourself if you're happy?"

"Happiness isn't always that great. My parents work all the time. They spend time with me, but sometimes they're just too busy. They're always pushing me to make friends. My doctor agrees it's supposedly the best thing for me. Stop me being an introvert."

"I suppose there's lots of kids like that."

"Probably is. But I'm not them. They're not me. They might handle it better. This," she indicated her arm, "makes me feel like things are real."

"What do you mean? Of course things are real. What else would they be?"

"If that's the case, why do I always feel like I'm walking around in a cloud? A big stormy one? Why does it feel like there's lightning and rain hitting me all the time?"

Wendy glanced up, a ridiculous move to see if a cloud really was positioned above the other's head. There wasn't, which she should have known. Did know.

"You're just… different," she said. "I am too."

"Maybe I am, but maybe I don't want to be. Cutting myself just lets the pain out a bit."

"Pain lets pain out? That doesn't make sense."

"Not to you, with your perfect life. You can still smile and hurt, you know."

"I do know!" Wendy snapped. "My parents act like they don't want me. They always have. I'm their slave. My dad, who's not really my dad anyway, is nasty and my mum drinks vodka like water. If anything happens with me, they treat it like it's an inconvenience. Like I'm one."

"I didn't know. I know what happened to you before, but still… you hide all that well."

"Me?" Wendy gasped incredulously.

She didn't talk about her home life or the issues she'd faced previously, but thought the way she was an obvious outsider made it clear she had… issues. She was dragged along by life's current and couldn't help feeling, most of the time, she was drowning. And her parents were waiting for the chance to put their feet on her head to keep her under.

"Well, yeah," Lisa said. "Nobody knows anything about you. You can recreate yourself. Tell people anything and they wouldn't know it wasn't true. I'd help. Back you up."

"Why? Why do you care?"

"Why not?" Lisa shrugged her shoulders and tilted her head to the side. "You're my friend."

"You really are shit at this friends stuff. You don't just tell someone they're your friend. It doesn't work like that."

"Well, we're getting on, aren't we?"

It was Wendy's turn to shrug.

"I suppose so."

"So, are you going to show me what you've got there?"

Wendy jumped slightly. She'd forgotten about their deal. Lisa had shared a secret and now it was her turn. She didn't want to, but knew there was no choice. Sharing Curious and, no doubt, Wonder, didn't just reveal she kept a dead hamster in a box. It would let Lisa know she had unusual ideas about life and death and friendship. Lisa could be disgusted. It could be Pagan all over again, with Wendy's meagre reputation trampled once more.

OK.

OK…

Deep breath.

OK…

She moved aside, wordlessly. Lisa stepped forward and peered into the box. Her face showed the repulsion Wendy knew would come, but then it changed to curiosity.

"What is… was it?"

"Curious."

"Yes, that's why I asked."

Wendy laughed an embarrassed snigger.

"No, his name is Curious."

"And Curious is…?"

"He's my pet. My friend."

Lisa's brow furrowed.

"Erm… How?"

"He's my friend. Easy."

"But he's dead."

"I know."

"So, how can he be your friend?"

Wendy thought about it. How did she make the other girl see? How did she do it without making herself sound crazy? She knew that's what it probably sounded like to others, even though it wasn't. To talk about Curious, she'd have to talk about Wonder. One led into the other. It would make understanding easier.

"My parents bought me a hamster," she began.

The story was easier to tell than she realised. It flowed from her in a release of pent up anguish. Of hatred. Of love. To Wendy, it all made complete sense. To Lisa, Wendy didn't know how it all came across. She could only tell what happened and how she felt. What the other made of it all was probably going to be revealed very soon.

"OK," said Lisa once Wendy had finished.

"Yes."

"So, you've got two dead hamsters for friends. One, your dad killed and the other you did so he couldn't."

"Yes…"

"You put one in Bradley, but got rid of the body when it was gone too much, but his spirit is still there."

"Her spirit, but yes."

"And this is the other one?"

"That's right."

"Cool."

"Cool?"

"Yeah. You've got friends who won't leave you. Or betray you."

"That's right. Friends forever."

"Like you and me," Lisa said, smiling.

So, she didn't run off. She didn't call Wendy a lunatic. She still wanted to be friends!

"Yes," Wendy said.

Lisa had won her over. If the girl could hear everything Wendy had told her and still wanted to be friends, how could she be denied?

"Would you like to come to mine for tea tomorrow night, after school?"

Wendy's eyes opened wide, but she managed to turn her head so the shocked expression wouldn't be seen.

"Sure, why not?"

"Good," said Lisa. "I have to go now. See you tomorrow?"

"See you tomorrow."

Wendy's smile, which remained all the way back to her mother's, was short lived.

"You've got no chance," Carol said without looking up from the television.

Wendy knew better than to argue with either parent. She also knew the woman wouldn't notice her absence after school. She'd asked for permission to go to Lisa's out of courtesy. It was an automatic response to the mother daughter dynamic. A child asked before doing. Wendy had asked. She'd been denied, but wouldn't let that stop her. If there was a chance Carol would actually be conscious and see her daughter wasn't home on time, Wendy would have acquiesced. In reality, she'd be back well before consciousness returned. The suggestion of going to a friend's house would be forgotten. It was, most likely, already.

Wendy went through to the kitchen. The smile Lisa gave her and her mother removed as if it had been an ugly stain, returned. As she cooked their own evening meal, she wondered what Lisa's mother would be serving the next night. What was it like to eat at someone else's house? How was she supposed to behave? How would it be being around parents who loved their child?

She was excited to find out. She had resisted Lisa's friendship and thought the way the girl pushed it was odd, but her reaction to Wendy's forest friends couldn't have been better. She'd accepted it easily, as if there was nothing out of the ordinary in having dead hamsters as friends.

Which, of course, there wasn't.

29 THEN

Lisa's house was smaller than Wendy's father's.

She lived in it with both parents and a younger brother. Benjamin was twelve and had a bouncy personality Wendy imagined could be tiring over time. He looked up to his sister, something evident from the way he spoke to her and seemed to feel the need to be always in the same room as her. Lisa didn't notice, or didn't show it. She was pleasant to him and didn't treat him as a nuisance, and otherwise ignored him.

Lisa's parents were immediately welcoming. Her mother, Katherine, hugged Wendy while her father, Keith, asked if their visitor would like a drink. Both of them gave Lisa a hug and a kiss. They asked about her day. They calmly reprimanded Benjamin for leaving his school bag at the bottom of the stairs. He picked it up and put it away with a smile and an apology.

The meal, cooked by Katherine and served by Keith, was delicious. It was easily the best food Wendy had tasted in as long as she could remember. And, they had dessert! She'd never had pudding, as Benjamin and Keith called it, before. Yes, she'd had cakes and ice creams and so on, but not many and never as an addendum to a main course. When she asked if she had to take out her plate and do the washing up, she was told no. She shouldn't worry about it. Why didn't she and Lisa go up to Lisa's room and relax for a little while before she had to go home?

Wendy felt at home. This was what families were meant to be like! Why couldn't her home – homes – be like this? Why did her parents have to be so... Wendy couldn't think of a word that would fit. Carol and Eddie were not nice people. They didn't deserve a child, and certainly didn't want one. It should be so easy for them to treat her the way Lisa's parents treated her. Wasn't it how families were meant to be?

Lisa's room was a decent size. Hers was an equal size to that of the adults in the house. Benjamin had the 'box room', so called because it was the smallest – box sized. It wasn't that small, of course. You could fit quite a few boxes in there, and a single bed, desk and a chest of drawers. Lisa's was decorated fairly plainly, with a dark cream paint covering the floors and a lighter shade on the ceiling. The carpet was a dark grey and the furniture was pine. It didn't really all go together, but even its disjointed aspect was more cohesive than anything in Wendy's room. Lisa admitted she didn't care what her room looked like. Her time, she said, wasn't spent staring at the décor. She was reading. She did her homework.

She made her own friends.

"You won't tell," Lisa said quietly. "Will you?"

"Tell about what?"

"Just promise first."

Wendy wouldn't. She had no one to tell whatever it was Lisa was referring to anyway. They'd already shared things neither wanted anyone else to find out about. Trust was already inferred in anything they did.

"I promise."

Lisa crouched next to her bed and reached under. She brought out a white shoebox not unlike the one Wendy kept Curious in. Placing it on the bed, she slowly lifted the lid. Unknowingly mimicking Lisa's actions in Dixon's Woods, Wendy looked inside.

Raisins?

In the bottom of the box, which was layered with strips of toilet roll, were round, black balls of various small sizes. To Wendy, they appeared to be raisins. Or sultanas, maybe. She could never tell the difference.

She looked closer and realised what they were.

Spiders. They were spiders, except they had no legs.

She didn't have to ask why Lisa would do this. Because of Wonder and Curious, she knew.

"Friends?"

Lisa grinned and nodded.

"That's right. I knew you'd know."

Time was short. Too short. By the time Lisa had introduced her friends and explained that she, too, was lonely and she, too killed creatures to ensure they didn't leave – though it was put in a less bloodthirsty way – Wendy needed to leave. She thought about staying for longer, but her mother would be waking up soon. If Wendy wasn't there, questions would be asked. Punishments would be handed out and the chances of her being able to see Lisa anytime soon, or to visit Wonder and Curious, were slim.

Both Lisa and her mother embraced her before she left. Keith said it had been an absolute pleasure having her there and she was welcome as much as she liked.

Wendy felt almost giddy walking home. She really wasn't used to people being so good to her. Or each other. In her world, those things just didn't happen. Being friends with Lisa would, at least, mean she would be exposed to it on a, hopefully, regular basis. She knew her initial reticence at agreeing to the friendship was so she wouldn't be hurt again. She wouldn't have to trust again. It had nothing to do with how nice or deserving of a Wendy's acceptance Lisa was. She was pleased to have been proven wrong. She looked forward to how their relationship could develop. She'd never had a best friend before! It was exciting!

And it did develop. Though Wendy never took Lisa home, the two rapidly became inseparable. Wendy even allowed her friend to take her box of legless spiders to Dixon's Woods. They'd be company for Curious and Wonder, with a few being scattered at both locations.

Having more creatures to visit meant the girls spent an increased amount of time in the woods. They weren't bothered by the noise or attentions of other children who might recognise them, as they would be if they went to the People's Park in the centre of town. The world was so distant once they were in the thick of the trees. The sounds of the nearby road faded, smothered by the foliage helpfully keeping it away from them.

It was on one trip to see Curious and the spiders, which sounded like a rock group to Wendy, they had the chance to increase their group.

They'd reached the clearing, which was larger now there were two of them going. They'd flattened the grass and uprooted a number of the smaller bushes. A couple of trees encroached on their den, but they forgave them. They even included the elms in their conversations sometimes, asking the bark's opinion on matters something that had lived for a hundred years or more might be versed in. A response was never forthcoming, but it would be rude not to ask.

Lisa had taken the lid off Curious' box, which Wendy didn't mind even though the hamster was her pet, not Lisa's. Wendy took it from her and placed it to one side. They both looked in. There was very little of Curious left and his decomposition had dampened the base of the box, disintegrating part of it. It was doing its best to remain together, though, which the girls were thankful for. The Raisins, the name both girls gave to the legless spiders, had yet to begin their disappearing act so were still there in their entirety, or their less than entire entirety.

A rustling in the closest bush to Curious' home startled them. The rustling stilled then began again. A whiskered snout poked from the leaves causing Lisa to squeal. The snout was followed quickly by a thick body and long tail. Wendy cried out, more shocked yell than fearful scream. Lisa grabbed a branch laid on the floor of the clearing from when she'd picked it up near the entrance to the woods a while before, using it to slash at the leaves blocking her way. It had made her feel like an intrepid explorer. She'd been ready to face and do battle with any mighty creatures that might attack them as they progressed through the jungle.

Now, there was no jungle or mighty beasts. There was a group of trees, two girls and a rat. Instinctively, she swung down on the back of the animal. It made a high pitched squeak as its back was broken, but still it tried, and failed, to move.

Lisa and Wendy stared at each other.

Lisa hadn't really meant to hurt the rat. She'd intended to scare it off. Rats were different to spiders. Wendy had killed a boy. It was in self defence, of course, but he was now dead. She'd deliberately taken Curious' life. Lisa was somewhat in awe of her friend, but killing something more than an arachnid hadn't occurred to her.

Until now..

30 THEN

Wendy reached out for the branch. The rat couldn't be left like that. Its life was crawling from its body slowly, and it was obviously suffering. Weak whines were the only sound it could make and they were fading as did it.

Lisa shook her head.

No. She'd done that. It was her responsibility.

She raised the branch, now a club and smashed it against the rat's head. The skull split, exposing its inner treasures. Lisa didn't notice. She hit it again. Again. She started to laugh, to cheer as she repeatedly struck the animal, battering it.

Wendy joined in the laughter. She was clapping her hands in time to Lisa's strikes. Jumping about.

Lisa stopped when she saw the pulped mess that had been the rat. She stared at it, dropping to her knees, panting. Wendy ceased her celebrations too, kneeling next to the other girl. Was Lisa going to cry? Would she hate herself for what she'd just done?

No!

"That was so cool!" she exclaimed.

"I know!" Wendy agreed, smiling broadly.

Lisa took Wendy's hand and gripped it tightly. She had a manic expression on her face, wide eyed with her mouth a wider slash than Wendy's.

"Can we do that again?" she asked. "Can we?"

Wendy nodded enthusiastically. Oh yes! They had to! Wendy couldn't have done that to either Wonder or Curious, but to an anonymous pest that spread disease? Without a doubt!

Traps. They needed traps. And something better than a random stick. A more substantial weapon. A cricket bat, in brand new condition, though it was a number of years old and had never been used. A hammer, the shaft of which had been replaced with a longer piece of wood by Lisa's father for when he was attaching Christmas lights to the outside of their garage, but hadn't had his loaned step ladders back from his brother.

Their first forays into trapping animals were a failure. They dug a hole and covered it, but the animal, another rat, easily escaped. They tried to hide and jump out when something scurried into their camp. Their leaps were more like untidy scrambles and, again, their potential victim escaped.

The girls became more thoughtful in their attempts. They took their time setting up more intricate designs, realising rushing just wasn't effective. After a number of abortive disappointments, which they didn't let deter them, finally, they saw success.

A clumsy combination of a forked stick, some string and a sack, plus a blob of peanut butter, resulted in shrieks of delight as the trap was tripped.

It was bigger than the rat, definitely. Stronger too. The sack, tied to a tree, was being yanked from side to side as the creature within fought to free itself. Wendy and Lisa stood over it, watching the movements with trepidation. And excitement.

They were about to halt the movements. Halt the whimpering. Halt the breathing. Halt the life.

They raised their weapons.

The rain of attacks hammered onto the sack for more time than it felt or was needed. The bat and hammer were much better suited to the task and gave the friends a greater sense of power and strength. Sweat stood proud on each of their brows and they shared the same look on their faces. They were lost in the moment, finding the pummelling exhilarating. All movements had ceased within the sack. Blood soaked into the material rapidly.

Wendy was reminded of the time she'd knocked over her mother's can of dark fruits cider. It spread across the carpet in a similar fashion. Wendy had been fascinated by the way the liquid looked to be leaping from fibre to fibre, racing across the floor to an unseen finish line, each droplet desperate to best those next to it.

Her fascination was short lived, with her father's hand smacking the back of her head returning her to the trouble she was in. Her mother had lost her temper in a way Wendy hadn't seen before. Not from the potential damage to the carpet, which an hour of cleaning by Wendy had ensured wouldn't happen. She was angry because of the loss of her alcohol. Cider didn't grow on trees, the girl was told.

She knew enough to keep the thought that yes, it actually did, to herself.

The bruise from the slap her mother gave her was hidden by her blouse. The swollen lip, from tripping next to her father, of course, was visible but went away soon enough. There'd been a few questions, as there would be. Nothing excessive. Nothing too prying. When the swelling disappeared, so did the curiosity, which had been only mild anyway.

The memory stalled her onslaught, though it took longer for Lisa to stop. The friend's hair was as wild as her eyes. Both hands were gripping the handle of the hammer, clenched around it as if to ensure it couldn't escape her grasp. Wendy didn't think it would go anywhere. It would have enjoyed the attack immensely. Lisa's barely contain fervour washed away the memory of her parent's cider related reaction. Wendy was back in the forest again.

"What do you think it is?" Lisa asked excitedly.

"What it was, don't you mean?" Wendy responded. "It's not an 'is' anymore."

Lisa laughed a little too hysterically. Wendy joined in, her own giggling just as manic and as genuine.

Once their hilarity had subsided, they carefully approached the sack. Neither believed there was any life still left in the trapped animal. There couldn't be. The misshapen mass and soaked material were testament to that.

"So, what do you think it was?"

Wendy shrugged. There'd been minimal noise and whatever it was hadn't been given the chance to announce its identity before…

"A fox, maybe?"

Lisa nodded. That's what she'd been thinking herself. She quite liked foxes. They were cute, though could be noisy when they screamed in the middle of the night. Sometimes, one would pass through her back garden on its way to wherever foxes went. Did they party until the early hours? Hunt witches? Go shopping? Where would they put their wallets or purses if so?

Killing one, however, didn't bother her at all. Her father had told her to keep away from them when they were in the garden. Foxes carried diseases, possibly in the same place as their purses (not her father's thought). They were pests who shit everywhere and killed other animals, like their neighbour's chickens, for fun rather than food.

Perhaps Lisa, herself, was part fox?

Wendy bent over and pinched the edge of the sack between her finger and thumb. She started to lift it slowly.

"Benji!"

"Shit!"

The second voice belonged to Lisa, but the first came from outside of their camp.

"Benji."

It was a man's voice. Not old but adult. The girls looked at each other frantically. Wendy dropped the sack's hem and they both ducked down.

"Benji! Come here boy!"

A dog. The man was looking for his pet. Calling for it.

It wasn't answering. Wendy pointed at the sack and mouthed the word 'dog'. Lisa frowned and nodded. Wendy gingerly held the sack again and started to lift it up.

"Benji! Where are you?"

The cloth was dropped. The duck became a low crouch. Breaths and hands were held as the pair clung to each other. Footsteps crunched fallen leaves, the sound moving closer.

"Benji?"

The man stopped just beyond the circle of trees surrounding them. They could hear his breathing and were sure he could hear their thudding heartbeats. He was going to find them. He must. It was obvious. He'd turn in their direction and walk straight into the camp. He'd see the friends. He'd see their weapons. The bloodied sack. He'd look inside. He'd know.

He probably knew already. He was just waiting, figuring out what he was going to do to the person responsible for his dear pet's death. How about exactly what was done to Benji? How about that?

Wendy was desperate to stand up. To apologise. Tell him she was sorry! They got carried away. They didn't really mean to hurt Benji. They didn't know it was a pet. They thought it was a rat. Or a fox. They were scared. No, of course it wasn't a trap. It was... It was...

What was it?

"BENJI!" Pause. "Stupid damn mutt. Gets on my bloody nerves."

The urge to announce their presence instantly left Wendy. The voice had a harsh edge. One that told her he'd be more than angry at them for killing his dog. Not only that, he'd be more than angry at his dead dog for getting itself killed. She began to tremble and was relieved to feel a similar tremor in her friend's hands.

"Well, I hope you know your way home, you little shit."

The leaf crunching footsteps began again, receding further into the forest. The man could be heard muttering to himself, swearing at the dog he'd never see again, even if it did know its way home. When he was finally gone, the girls collapsed onto the ground. They were laid on their backs, eyes closed, waiting for their hearts and breathing to calm.

They looked at each other and held the gaze for a moment. Lisa was the first to break, the snigger popping a small snot bubble in her left nostril. Wendy didn't notice, as the barely stifled laugh of her friend prompted a much larger and far less restrained one in herself. This, in turn, released the full force of Lisa's mirth and, in seconds, both were lost in a fit of hysterical laughter. While one was holding her stomach, the other was banging her fist down onto the earth. While one's laugh had turned into gasping coughs of merriment, the other's had lifted an octave and become a stream of breathless hee hee hees.

Slowly, they calmed down. Still on their backs, eyes closed, they allowed their gasps to become breaths. Their hands brushed against each other, and they both took hold. The girls remained that way until the light began to fade and they realised they needed to get home, but had yet to inspect their prize. Still holding hands, they moved to the bloodied sack.

Wendy reached cautiously forward. She knew the dog would be dead, and it wouldn't leap out at her, snarling and biting. It wouldn't, either, be laying whimpering, staring at her with beseeching eyes. So why be careful? Was she scared? Now the adrenaline that fuelled the attack had dissipated, was she feeling guilty?

No. Her concern was that she might be disappointed. What if it didn't look right? If it appeared to be simply sleeping? If it was still alive and was looking up at them with a semi-crushed head and one swollen, bloodshot eye?

If it was any of those things, would they be able to attack it again? Once it was seen, it was real. While it was concealed in the sack, it could be anything at all, even though they knew exactly what it was. They could lie to themselves. A dog was different to a fox, too. It wasn't just an animal.

Besides, if it wasn't dead, it wouldn't be able to be their friend.

Lisa squeezed her hand in support. It told Wendy that she was strong. She could do this. It also told her to get a move on. The light was fading and excitement could quickly turn to fear in a dark forest with a dead dog.

31 THEN

Soaked, congealing blood meant the sack didn't lift easily.

When Wendy tried to raise the edge, it didn't immediately move. She pulled up harder, and grimaced at the sticky, slurping sound the material made as it separated from the dead animal. She looked at Lisa and saw it was affecting her friend the same way. Gulping down her nerves, and bile, she yanked it up.

The tackiness reminded her of a plaster being removed and she felt sorry for the dog. It would have suffered enough pain whilst being bludgeoned to death. Now, it should be spared anything further. She mentally apologised and sent soothing thoughts the animal's way.

The misshapen lump of bloodied fur looked nothing like she assumed Benji would have had it been still alive enough to wag its tail.

No, not 'it.' He.

"It's a bit messy," Lisa said.

"He is," Wendy replied, not emphasising the pronoun, but hoping its inclusion was heard. "But at least he'll be with us, now. His owner sounded a bit of a dick."

"Yeah," Lisa agreed. "He's the stupid damned mutt, not Benji!"

"No, the poor thing was probably abused. We've saved him, now."

"Yeah," Lisa repeated. "He won't have to take any of that anymore. He can stay here with us."

Wendy smiled. She was so pleased Lisa had the same thought as her. The dog wasn't just an animal they'd killed. He was a new friend. Someone for Wonder and Curious to play with. Although she was extremely happy with her hamsters, she would have loved to have a dog welcoming her home, all waggy tail and licks.

"What do we do with it now?" Lisa asked.

Wendy stared at Benji, ignoring the 'it' and trying to come up with an answer. Killing the dog was an amazing feeling, without a doubt. It had been an exhilarating rush of feelings and emotions, muddled together so she was unsure which was which. They'd expected to capture a rat. Maybe a squirrel. Something smaller. The dog was much better! It had taken them a good three rungs further up the ladder of potential victims than they'd intended. Given them an experience they knew they'd have to repeat. A rat would be an anti-climax after that.

"Bait," she said, finally.

"Bait? What do you mean?"

"Well, what's the best way to lure other animals?"

Lisa didn't respond, her brow furrowed. Then realisation dawned and she grinned.

"Bait!"

"Exactly. We use Benji, or what's left of him, to bring other animals. Then we… let them join our family."

"Perfect!"

"That's what I thought," Wendy said.

"Wouldn't it be better if we could, sort of, spread it out?"

"What do you mean?"

"Well, it's a lot of dog and he won't last for that long. If we can't get back here for a few days, he might be all gone and we'll have nothing."

"True," Wendy nodded. She thought for a moment, and could see an answer, but it wouldn't be pleasant. "We could chop him up?"

"Do what?"

"Well, if we chopped him up and just left bits of him, he'd last longer. He'd be helping us more too."

"Great idea, except how do we chop up a dog, and what do we do with the bits we haven't used yet?"

"We'll have to come back tomorrow. I'll bring the saw from under the sink. And some gloves. Do you have, like, a cool box or something?"

"Your saw is under your sink? In the kitchen."

Wendy nodded.

"Don't ask me."

"OK, well, we've got a cooler for picnics and camping. It's in the garage."

"Would it be missed?"

"Well, Dad's working all hours at the minute, so we won't be going on holiday anytime soon, I'd say."

"Could you get hold of it without him seeing?"

"Definitely."

So, a plan was made. The light was fast fading, but they were feeling alight.

"We'll have to be back early," Lisa pointed out. "A load of animals come out at night. They'll make a right meal of him."

"They will," said Wendy. "I suppose we could... twag it?"

"Twag it? Really? I've never cut school before. What if we get caught?"

Wendy didn't want to think about what might happen if her parents discovered she had missed school. Even if they didn't care, they'd pretend they did, just so they could dole out some punishment. But, if she didn't do so, they'd probably have to start again as, by tomorrow evening, there might not be much of Benji left. Killing another animal didn't bother her, in fact she welcomed the feelings it brought, but the dog was a... a gift! It gave them so much potential for more friends to be made!

"I think we should let Benji help us. I think he'd like that."

"OK," sighed Lisa. "You win."

"We can use some rat poison on him. Let the other animals eat him, with the poison, and that'll make it easier for us."

"Good thinking! Even if they don't all die here, or close by, some will."

"Exactly!"

Wendy had a thought, one she wasn't sure Lisa would go for, but it seemed too irresistible not to voice.

"We could make a cemetery for them."

"Huh?"

"We could bury them all here. I got rid of Wonder, because she was there all the time anyway. You saw what I did with Curious. If we buried them, it could be like a... a creche. Or a home. Their graves could be their rooms."

"It'd give them something they could have as their own?"

"Yes!"

"Let's do it then," Lisa said.

Wendy could barely contain her excitement. She'd never had a real friend, outside of her hamsters, and to find one who shared her ideas and ideals was something she never believed could happen. She pulled Lisa close and embraced her. Lisa returned the hug and, with neither thinking about it, they kissed.

It lasted for a second only, and the girls hastily pulled away from each other, releasing both the embrace and their still held hands. Both kept their eyes on Benji, not knowing how to respond to what just happened.

"We need to get home. It'll be properly dark by the time we get there."

"Yeah. OK. Erm… see you tomorrow."

"Tomorrow. Yeah."

The girls moved quickly through the trees, back towards the road, without speaking. They told themselves it was because they needed to concentrate on their path through the forest in the twilight. It was treacherous, and they each tripped multiple times. When they were beyond the trees, they walked back to the main road, still silent. By the time it came to part ways, they had yet to say another word and parted with just a nod.

Wendy had a restless night sleep. She wouldn't allow herself to dwell on why that might be and kept her thoughts focussed on Benji and what he could bring them in death. By the time they were finished, they'd have so many friends, their forest hideaway would be crowded.

A little like her thoughts.

When morning came, Wendy was still tired and struggled to get herself moving. Shouts of 'Shift it!' and 'Get bloody out of here, girl!' succeeded in motivating her, however. She slipped out, taking the saw, gloves and rat poison with her, easily.

Her trip back to the forest was slower than usual. She hoped Lisa would be there, but part of her wished she wouldn't be.

She was.

"Morning," Wendy said, as brightly as she could.

"Morning, Wendy," Lisa responded.

Her enthusiasm sounded sincere. Wendy didn't know if her own had, but she was going to do her best and ignore the awkwardness. The adventure before them was too important to worry about anything else.

"Have you checked Benji?"

Lisa shook her head.

"Not yet. I wanted to wait for you to get here first. We need to be doing this together."

Wendy smiled at that. Whatever had happened, Lisa was putting their reason for being there first.

"Come on, then," she said, feeling more at ease.

She could see the sack had been disturbed and, on one side, a hole had been chewed through. Not just in the material, either.

The ribs of Benji's chest were visible.

32 THEN

Wendy licked her lips.

The sight of the dog's innards, for ribs were joined by an open tear chewed into its stomach, hadn't made her hungry, but it had fed a hunger. And increased it.

She resisted the urge to dip her finger into the holes. It was not only the temptation to feel what the inside of an animal felt like, but possibly to taste it too that she fought. Lisa, though, was not so reticent. She inserted her own index finger into the stomach cavity and pulled it out slowly.

Lisa and Wendy both looked closely at the congealed slime that coated the digit. Wendy sniffed it but, before she could really tell if there was a smell, let alone what that might be like, Lisa moved her hand forward as if to wipe it on her friend's face.

Wendy swore and pulled back, while the other girl laughed.

"I wasn't going to really!"

"Well, I didn't know that," said Wendy trying to appear angry even though she wasn't.

"It feels weird," Lisa said.

"Like what?"

"Like... sort of warm and wet. Lumpy bits that feel like they're trying to hold on to me."

"Ugh!"

Wendy was pleased she'd been able to refrain from doing what Lisa had. She wasn't squeamish, clearly, but it didn't sound at all pleasant. If, she thought, they were going to continue on this path, she would probably need to get over her reservations. If, indeed, they were going to continue with their current plan, she'd have to.

While Lisa wiped her finger on a large leaf, Wendy bent forward and copied her friend. She didn't immediately pull her finger out.

Lisa was right. It did feel strange, though not as disgusting as she'd imagined. The 'lumpy bits', no doubt organs or intestines, did seem to be trying to keep a hold of her, but that would be simply the effect of the viscous surfaces sticking to her skin.

It wasn't unpleasant. In fact, it was veering on pleasant.

"I knew you wouldn't be able to help yourself!" Lisa exclaimed. "'Orrid isn't it?"

Wendy nodded to disguise her disagreement. She'd quite liked it.

Thankfully, there was still plenty of Benji left to serve their needs. Whatever had dined on his corpse must have been either small enough to be full on the little they'd consumed, or been scared off by their approach. Either way, the dog was mostly intact.

"How do we do this?" Lisa asked, removing the lid from the cool box she'd brought along.

Wendy hefted the saw. She'd been worried about whether or not she'd be able to go through with the next step. Now, after feeling Benji's insides, she was actually looking forward to it. There'd be minimal blood flow now, as most of the contents of the dog's veins had seeped out, to be soaked up by the sack and the ground. That would make it easier. Now…

Deep breath.

Now, she'd just have to imagine she was breaking up old furniture for the 'Bommie' Night bonfire. Guy Fawkes Night was still months away, of course, and Wendy had never had the chance to be involved in the bonfire construction. This was her chance, in a way.

No.

Benji didn't deserve that. He'd been a loyal pet to an owner who hadn't appreciated him. The least they could do was make up for that.

Wendy wasn't going to be cutting up a rickety chair. She was going to be dismembering and beheading a dog. The excitement of the previous day, when they'd collectively beaten the life from the animal, had been invigorating. Now came the dirty part of it. Though she knew Benji would want this – to help them and be a part of their family – she was still nervous about chopping him up.

There was no turning back, though. If she, or they, did change their minds, Benji wouldn't stay around. He'd be off looking for someone he could trust. Wendy wouldn't blame him, either. Nor would she blame any other animals they killed if they did the same.

No, it was time.

"Here we go," she said.

Lisa was watching intently. She leaned forward with eyes wide as if preparing to unwrap her favourite Christmas present.

Wendy gingerly placed her hand on Benji's shoulder. She knew he wasn't going to move, but that didn't mean she couldn't be careful to avoid waking him. She planned to begin with removing his head. It was how she ate Jelly Babies, so seemed the most obvious starting point. The saw blade was resting on the dog's neck, ready to stroke the fur. The flesh. The bones.

She began to move her hand forward and backwards. At first, the serrations were pulling at the skin rather than cutting it, but Wendy was undeterred. She knew it would take effort and wouldn't necessarily go smoothly. Quickly, she was through and, eventually, hitting bone. This was harder, and the saw didn't seem to be putting up a decent fight against it, scraping over rather than through.

She had to stop.

"What's wrong?" Lisa asked.

"It's not going through. The bone is too hard."

"Can't you just, like, saw harder? Or maybe faster?"

"I've tried. It's not working."

She'd expected the bone to be brittle, like the chicken bones after the rare Sunday lunches she'd enjoyed. It was just a dog, not a person. It wasn't like she had to cut into a femur. She'd chosen the neck. Shouldn't that have been easy? Going through the joints so the only tough parts were tendons or muscles?

Ah.

The spine.

"If I saw," she said, "can you push down on the blade? Give it some weight?"

Lisa hesitated before agreeing. The girl was enjoying being a part of this, but was happy to let Wendy do the hard stuff. Killing was one thing. That was simple, and immensely enjoyable. This seemed to be worse. Still, she supposed she had to do some of the dirty work. It was only fair.

She pulled a number of leaves from the nearest bushes and layered them in her palms before pushing down on the top edge of the saw blade. She could feel Wendy's breath, warm against her cheek. It felt nice. Wendy began to move the tool forwards, but the weight of her friend made it a difficult task.

"Just ease off a bit so I can get it going," she said.

She looked up and caught her breath at the other's unexpected proximity. There was a moment that hung on the still air as if not knowing which way to move, then Lisa coughed and stood back up.

"OK. If you think you can do it."

"Well, I can try. It just needs a bit more effort, that's all."

"OK. Let's go again."

They resumed their earlier position, with Lisa putting a few inches of distance between their faces. It meant she was crouching awkwardly, and she almost fell when Wendy started to move again.

It was slow going at first. The dog's neck was resisting the insistence that it be disconnected from the torso. Eventually, as the girls found a rhythm, it realised battered, brittle bones were no match for the cold steel of a serrated blade. With relief, the saw made it through and thudded to the ground on the other side of the animal.

"Yes!" Wendy exclaimed, dropping the saw and clapping her hands.

Lisa echoed the sentiment and punched the air.

"Brilliant!" she said, reaching to pick up Benji's head.

As she lifted it, she swore. The neck and shoulder, or what was left of them, were raising up too. If she hadn't seen the reason why, she would have screamed, thinking he was getting up to go for his morning walk, regardless of his deceased nature. Wendy didn't quite scream, but she did stumble back, her imagination flashing through her mind faster than reason.

Lisa giggled.

"He won't bite! It's just a bit of skin that's still attached, that's all."

"I knew that," said Wendy, blushing. "I was just messing."

"Yeah, right. I bet."

Lisa put her foot on Benji's shoulder and yanked the head up. It came away easily, the thread of flesh knowing it wouldn't be able to cling on any longer. She spun the head in her hand and pushed the muzzle towards her friend.

"Gizza kiss!"

Wendy pulled back and swatted Lisa's hand. Benji's head flew through the air and hit the ground. It rolled twice and was stopped by a slight hollow in the earth.

Benji was staring at them. He didn't look amused.

33 THEN

Cutting up a dead dog is not an easy task.

The bones of such an animal prefer not to be severed, so the work must be carried out at the joints. Shoulders. Pelvis. Neck, of course. The main body was a problem, but the friends worked together to separate vertebrae and snap ribs.

Finally, Benji was in pieces and at peace. Lisa and Wendy were dirty and bloody and sweating. They were also relieved and very pleased with themselves. The dog had been fully taken apart and was, more or less neatly, arranged in piles of similar body parts. Legs with legs. Torso with torso. The organs were the difficult part. Neither girl had taken them into account, thinking they only had to contend with Benji's outer surface. When they realised, they shrugged and got to work pulling them all out. They found the slippery viscera oddly soothing to handle. Rather than simply slop it all onto another pile, they filled the sack they'd used to catch the dog in the first place to hold his innards.

As they'd planned, they filled the cool box with as much of the meat as they could. They were fairly unceremonious in the cramming of it in, as Benji wasn't going to mind. He wouldn't feel it anyway. There were a few pieces left, plus the organs, so they decided to leave a couple of sections of body out and hide the rest.

"We can let Wonder look after it," suggested Wendy. "Let her do what she wants."

"Erm…" Lisa wasn't sure.

How could the ghost of a hamster keep an eye on their prize? She didn't have any. It seemed the best idea, however. They needed to dish out the delicacies in a specific way to fulfil their plan. If Wonder failed in her task, as she suspected she would, it wouldn't matter too much. They had plenty to keep them going.

"OK," she agreed.

Wendy volunteered to take Benji's 'unwanted' parts across from Dixons to Bradley Woods. She did so quickly and carefully. The road that split the two forests was empty of cars, thankfully, so she hurried over and disappeared into Bradley.

When she reached Wonder's den, she had to apologise. She didn't know if dividing Benji would mean he would be in both locations at once. Would it diminish his presence in either? No. He would be over the road. That was where he died and that was where he would haunt.

She spoke briefly to her old pet, and apologised for the briefness of her visit. She'd be back as soon as was possible, she promised.

Back with Lisa, the pair were swift in preparing their next trap. A sack wasn't required now, as they had the bait they'd need. With a generous sprinkling of their rat poison condiment, the meal was set. Once done, they stepped back together.

"Looks good, right?"

"Definitely," Lisa agreed.

"We should go. Somehow we have to get cleaned up without our parents finding out."

"Didn't you bring a change of clothes?"

Wendy shook her head. She hadn't considered just how messy the task would be, so another set of clothes hadn't occurred to her. She would have to sneak back home without being seen, and also manage to sneak into the house. It would be incredibly difficult.

"Good job I did, just in case."

"You did?"

Lisa reached into a bag, which Wendy hadn't noticed until that point, and pulled out two sets of school uniform. She handed one over.

"I brought a second set because I was bringing one for me. I didn't know if you'd think about it."

"Thanks, that's great!"

Lisa shrugged, smiling. She'd also had the foresight to pack some moisture wipes to clean themselves with, and a bag to put used ones in for throwing away. She was always fairly methodical, and tending to think through every detail. What they were doing that day had brought up a number of unexpected variables, but mess wasn't one of them.

The girls cleaned their exposed skin - face, hands, legs etc. - and began to undress. They paused at the same moment and glanced nervously at each other. There was a nervous chuckle from one of them, and they turned their backs to one another to complete their changing.

They left the area, talking animatedly about the possibilities before them. Although they'd enjoyed, really enjoyed, killing Benji and welcoming him into their family, they needed a new method of building their circle of friends. Meat and poison were ideal. They could come back every day to see if anything had been caught, and dig a grave for those that had. If they were unsuccessful at any time, they'd spend the time meeting and interacting with all those who'd died before.

And so many came to visit!

The smell of decaying lunch seemed to be an attractive proposition. Whether the poison sprinkled on top and pushed deep into the meals helped with that, Wendy and Lisa didn't know. It certainly didn't put anyone off. Rats, two badgers, a deer, even. Creatures great and small dined on Benji's remains, then stayed long enough for their life to take its leave of their bodies. Rather than create a graveyard purely in the location of their camp, the friends chose to scatter them around. It meant there wasn't a crowd. There wasn't a collection of muddy mounds increasing the risk of discovery. The spirits wouldn't feel tied to one place, either. They would have the forest to caper about in, and the camp as a base.

At first, Lisa shared Wendy's pleasure. She enjoyed being surrounded by the ghosts of so many different animals, all with their own, individual personalities. Sombre and fun and serious and quirky and mischievous.

At first, Lisa shared Wendy's glee at each new addition. She would laugh. She'd chuckle. Smile. Applaud. It faded over time, however. Lisa's excuses to avoid returning to the woods became repetitive and, more often than not, Wendy would be there alone. It was the same at school. Lisa would be hurrying off to another class or her parents or an after school club.

At first, Wendy missed her friend terribly. She wished the kiss hadn't happened, as surely that was the reason the other girl was distancing herself. It was nothing. A mistake prompted by the rush of delight. It didn't mean either of them needed to be embarrassed by it.

But, Lisa was. Wendy, when she finally had the chance to be

alone with her friend, tried to find out why Lisa was ignoring her. Lisa denied it, which Wendy had expected. Life was getting in the way, that was all.

Except, that wasn't all. Lisa could hardly look Wendy in the eyes without having to quickly direct them anywhere else.

Over time, as the foxes, rats and, on occasion, deer visited Wendy and didn't leave, she found the solitude once more comforting. It was only the voice of a 'real' person she was missing. Someone to share her pleasure with. She still had the many spirits of the dead to keep her company.

It was a Tuesday when she discovered Lisa was changing schools. A little after lunch time. There had been a group huddled together, laughing. Wendy heard words such as 'dyke' and 'lezza'. She heard a lot more derogatory comments mixed in.

Lisa. She had admitted she liked girls. She'd kissed one and it had made her realise where her heart lay. Being different was a target on the back that few in the school would not take a shot at. It saddened Wendy that tolerance wasn't a class on the curriculum. It saddened her more that it felt as if their kiss had led to Lisa's realisation, thence her troubles.

As Lisa walked out of the building for the last time, she offered a half smile, one that combined apology and regret, and a brief wave. Wendy didn't have time to return them, as her friend was gone.

She never saw Lisa again, and kept herself away from any relationship that might develop into an actual friendship. The dead, killed at her hand, were all the company she needed, and she ensured those numbers increased. It was surprising to her how many animals she could find if she didn't simply sit and wait. The woods were large and teeming with life. Wendy took full advantage of the fact, and that meant she couldn't be hurt by people.

People lied, whether maliciously or not. It was a natural part of daily life, and Wendy hated it. Whether by exclusion, deliberation or thinking it was a kindness, a lie was still a lie. It was still not the truth. Yes, the truth could hurt, but knowing was better than not, wasn't it?

Animals didn't lie.

Nor did the dead.

The corpses rotted over the years. Her burial sites became more widespread, and she began to struggle finding new ones. Thankfully, eventually, she learned how to drive. Taking her hobby on the road gave her the ability to find new places to kill. She became... fuller. More whole. She felt complete, mostly. The small part of her that no amount of dead animals could fill was ignored. It was buried along with the friends she was making around the country.

34 THEN

The years after school were not uneventful.

Wendy's parents didn't speak to each other, not even about her, so if they weren't seeing her, they assumed she was at the other's house. She quickly learned to use this to her advantage. The rebellious nature that infiltrated her attitude to everything was entirely out of character, but she wore it like a warm blanket on a winter's night. It made her feel better.

Not the actual acts she did whilst wearing it, as such, but the ability to do them. She took pleasure in going against all she had been and all she suffered. The lack of love from her parents showed her that she, too, could bury her feelings. On her part, they were drowned in vodka and semen from endless booze fuelled nights and countless uninhibited sexual partners, only a few of which lasted more than the few moments of intimacy they shared.

Bradley was the one who brought her back to herself. He suggested to her that this path she'd taken was self-destructive. Sleeping rough. Washing in supermarket toilets. Theft and three, admittedly brief, incarcerations for shoplifting. It would only lead to an early demise or worse, a lifelong addiction to substances harder than alcohol and bodily fluids.

Bradley was kind, usually. She liked him and loved the way his name was a constant reminder of all her friends. Bradley wasn't the best looking young man in the neighbourhood, but he accepted Wendy not for what she had become, but for what she was beneath the harsh exterior. He saw through her anger. He heard her cry for help and answered it.

He was usually kind. Occasionally, and this was rarely, he fell into a dark mire for no other apparent reason than it was a cloudy day or it was Thursday instead of Friday and he had another day at work before the weekend began. As Bradley saw through Wendy's façade and invited her into his home, bringing her train back on track and preventing its derailment, she saw past his.

His smiles were genuine. His embraces would lift her feet from the ground while throwing her heart higher still. The death of his brother from the car that hit him when he stepped out into the street without looking, but didn't stop to see if the boy was injured – or dead – opened up random abysses in front of him he couldn't help stepping into. The fact he was standing next to his brother and was barely missed by the same car sometimes became a hand behind him to push him in.

Wendy and Bradley helped each other recover. She was grateful for that for the rest of her life. She would do anything for him, and did.

Wednesday evenings were for relaxation. The pair didn't have overly hectic lives, but Wednesday evenings were always set aside for doing nothing other than watching television and eating a nice meal together.

Coronation Street was never missed by Wendy, though Bradley wasn't as invested as his partner. She would need to shush him repeatedly as he asked who that was or what happened there. It became a game. The programme had just started, and she'd just told him to be quiet for the first time, when a scream, squeal and commotion from outside brought them running to their front door.

A car was driving at speed away from a group of people running to the middle of the road. They were surrounding a young boy. The way he was laying on the tarmac, like Geppetto's wooden son if his strings were cut too early, and his blank stare that seemed to look into the eyes of everyone there at once, while seeing none, showed he was dead.

Wendy turned to look at Bradley, but he was gone. She closed the door quietly and went to look for him. She knew. The dead boy had brought his brother's death to the forefront of his mind. She found him sitting on the top step of their stairway. He had a length of rope in his hands, with a neatly tied noose at one end. She sat down beside him quietly.

"Bradley," she said in a soft voice.

He didn't answer. He was staring into the space over the rail of the landing. Their house wasn't large, though it did have a decent sized entrance hall, allowing for stairs that bent at ninety degrees half way up. This created a void, one that had captured his attention.

"Bradley, love. Are you OK?"

He shook his head. She followed his gaze and stared into the same void, hoping she could bring him back from it.

"The... the poor boy. I'm sorry you saw that. And the car just drove off."

"No," Bradley said. His tone was normal. Conversational, as if the death hadn't just happened and they were waiting for the next episode of Coronation Street to begin. "The car didn't. The driver did. Someone killed that boy and just drove off."

"Yes, someone did. They won't get away with it."

"They will. They always did."

"Not always."

He looked at her for a moment before turning back to the space.

"Yes, always. They didn't catch Bobby's killer."

"You said they did. He gave himself up, didn't he?"

"I said that, didn't I?"

A pause, not one she wanted to interrupt.

"I lied. They didn't catch him. Not ever."

"But... OK... Why...?"

"Why did I say they did? I didn't want to think about them getting away with it. I told myself they gave themselves up out of guilt. They were sorry. But they weren't."

"I see." She held his hand, closing hers over his so she couldn't feel the rope. "What's this for?"

"It's a noose. It's for cleaning the windows."

"I don't think it will do a very good job, personally. How long have you had it?"

"Always."

Wendy had the urge to pull away from him, then. She hadn't known about it at all, and this surprised her. A noose was something that should have been difficult to hide. Surely, she'd have seen it at some point.

"Why?"

"Just in case, really. In case Bobby came back to haunt me. In case I decided I couldn't go on with the guilt. In case I wanted to swap places with him."

"You know none of that will bring him back, don't you?"

"Are you sure about that? How do you know?"

"It's not the way the world works. It's not that easy. Dead is dead."

"So you don't think I'll see him again when I die?"

"I don't know. Nobody does. But no, I don't think you will."

"You're wrong. I will, and that out there reminded me I need to see him again."

"What are you saying?"

"The noose. It's time for it to come out and play."

"Play? At what?"

"Strangle the brother."

"Wh..?"

Wendy let the start of the word hang in the air until it faded, dissipating like the breath Bradley was so eager to be rid of. She kept the last part of it inside her, trapping it with a craving she had ignored while being with him. She was so ready to try and persuade him to change his mind. Bobby wouldn't be waiting for him on the other side. She didn't think there was no other side, but wasn't sure of the form it would take. The only thing she felt certain of, was there'd be no past loved ones stood waiting. No cloud parties where the winged deceased celebrated your passing.

But, who was she to mess with his beliefs? She loved him. Shouldn't she be more supportive? And, if he insisted on speeding his journey to meet him, why couldn't she be willing to allow him? Talk him into it, even? Isn't that what someone who cared would do? Make him happy, even if that meant watching him die?

"OK," she said.

"OK? What do you mean."

"You've never been happy," Wendy said. "Not since then."

"That's not true. I've been happy with you."

"You've been happier, maybe, but not fully happy. I think part of you died with Bobby. I think you're not just looking to be reunited with your brother, but the rest of you, too. You want to be whole."

Bradley looked down at the noose and stroked the spiral knot with his thumb.

"Yes," he said quietly. "That's exactly what I want."

"So, OK."

"OK, what?"

"OK, I'll help you."

"You will, how? Why?"

"Because I want you to be happy. This will make you happy. I'll help you do it."

"You will?"

"Yes," Wendy said, her sadness losing the battle with her excitement. "I don't think you could do it yourself."

"No, maybe not."

"How, then?"

Wendy took the rope and tied the end to the top banister rail. She'd estimated the length needed to ensure Bradley would fall, but not touch the ground or the lower steps. It would be enough to snap his neck. It would be enough to kill him.

She indicated for Bradley to go to her, which he did, and she slipped the noose over his neck. No words were exchanged, and no sign of affection apart from a brief, awkward hug that was quickly released. She tapped the rail, indicating he should climb up which, again, he did. Wendy moved the noose to straighten it, much like the tie of a corpse being smartened up for its funeral. He looked down at it and smiled.

Bradley leaned forward and moved as if to push himself off, but hesitated. He attempted a second time to go, and still was unable to make the actual jump. He looked up and took a deep breath, then shook his head and turned to his partner, opening his mouth to speak.

Wendy's hard push ensured any words were choked off by the abrupt tightening of the noose around Bradley's neck. She saw his falling body jerk to a sudden halt at the end of the rope and heard what she assumed was the snapping of his neck.

"Hmmm. Effective. You died well, honey."

His body jerked a couple of times and the stench of his involuntary defecation rose up to assault her nostrils.

"Well, mostly."

Wendy turned and walked quickly down the stairs. She had to lean to the side to avoid Bradley's still swinging legs, but didn't look at him. She had a sudden longing to reconnect with Curious and her other friends. Bradley had been about to change his mind. She could tell.

She didn't need that negativity in her life. She had to look onwards and upwards now. Her partner had shown her that by his refusal to do so, and his impending choice to continue living would have prevented her from going anyway. She cared for him. She'd have stayed with him however he was. Bradley's suicide was a window opening onto a view of the world Wendy had not seen before. She could be away from any darkness. She could live her life. She could be back with her friends and make new ones, except she would find a way to stop them leaving her.

"Thank you," she said as she closed the front door behind her.

She would return later. She'd call the police to report, as the distraught lover she was, her beloved's death. And she would move on. And up.

35 THEN AND NOW

The day was refreshing. A light rain had eased the humidity. 'Muggy' was a word Wendy disliked, and she disliked even more that she used it because it fit so well.

Closing the garden gate behind her, she turned towards the bus stop. There was no immediate destination in mind, as yet. Eventually, she would make it back to her childhood home, then go back to Bradley and Dixon's Woods. A plan was forming, one that would mean her friends would no longer have to be present only in spirit. They could be there in form, too.

Her interest in the ancient Egyptian culture had taught her about their burial rituals. Mummification, in particular. Embalming techniques had moved on dramatically since those days, and funeral directors used them on a daily basis to make the dearly departed last a little longer for their families to visit.

What if….?

"Oh, excuse me!"

Wendy jumped. She hadn't noticed the man coming around the corner, and had almost collided with him.

"That's fine," she said, smiling. She felt like she would be smiling every day from that point on.

"May I say, you have a lovely smile?" the man said, nodding slightly.

"You may," Wendy replied without hesitation.

Boldly, the man turned and stepped in beside her as she resumed her walking.

"I'm Arthur," he said.

"I'm sure you are," she said.

###

Interruptions always niggled Wendy. It was the height of

rudeness and, even if the other person didn't know the one they were getting in touch with was busy, they should!

She looked at the ringing phone's screen. 'Genny 🩶 '

The heart indicated a loved one. A partner or daughter. She should answer it. If she didn't, Genny might keep calling, which would be even worse. Besides, didn't modern phones have some method of tracking them? It was the definition of mistrust, as far as she was concerned. Yes, the missing or stolen phone could be located, but didn't it mean husbands could check up on their wives, and vice versa? People's lives should be private, and even between couples, some secrets should be allowed, as long as they weren't destructive if ever discovered.

"Hello?" she said.

"Lee?" a woman's voice said.

She sounded common. Not uneducated, but not entirely educated, either.

"No, I found this phone. I was hoping to return it."

"Who the hell are you? Why is a woman picking up my Lee's phone? Is he messing about again? Has he told you I don't understand him? That's his favourite one. Well, I understand all too well, but whatever he told you is a lie. He's spoken for."

"I assure you, young lady, there is nothing going on between your Lee and myself." The word 'lady' was spoken through gritted teeth. Wendy was sure there was nothing ladylike about the woman. "I found this phone in the People's Park. I was waiting for someone to call it so I could return it to its owner. I haven't seen this Lee, and have no desire to!"

"Whatever. Just tell him to get his arse back here, right?"

"I said I don't know him, if you'd like to listen," said Wendy tensely. "Look, I'm a pensioner. I have no need or desire for any shenanigans with your Lee or anyone else. I was doing a good deed by trying to return this telephone. I can happily throw it in the bin and forget about it, or put it back where I found it and let some reprobate have it, if you'd prefer."

There was a moment of silence on the other end, which made Wendy smile. She would not be spoken to like that.

"I'm sorry," the woman said. "I didn't mean to have a go at you. He's not come home, so I was worried. I thought he might have hurt himself or had an accident."

Of course you did…

"That's fine. I would appreciate it if you think before launching your spite at random people in future."

"I beg your... I mean, no, of course. I'm sorry. Can I have the phone back, please? I don't want it to get lost again. He'll be pleased when he comes back."

Wendy, keeping her voice sharp enough to show she was still irate, but softening it a little in mock understanding, gave her address. The woman would come along in an hour or two to collect it, she said, along with three more apologies.

Wendy hung up the phone and set it down on the small table by the front door. She was looking forward to Lee's partner coming along for the phone, not knowing its owner was so close. She was sure he wouldn't want to see her. He was too good for her, and was well rid of the trollop.

She walked into the lounge, wondering if she should tell Lee he'd received the call. Would he want to know? Would Wendy herself? Wendy, herself, wouldn't want to be associated with a partner who acted like that, thank you very much. Still, she should probably tell him he might be in trouble when he got home.

If he got home.

Which he wouldn't.

Wendy smiled to herself. She liked looking after her guests. It made her days feel worthwhile. These were her friends. She wouldn't let any harm, physical or emotional, come to them.

She looked out of the window. The park was busy, filled with happy looking parents and joyful children. A woman was walking a dog. How lovely?

She began to turn away, but noticed a young man, dressed like those thugs she saw on television all the time, approaching the woman, who clearly didn't want to speak to him. The dog barked, drawing Wendy's attention and, when she looked back, the man was on the floor.

She rushed out, hurrying across the road towards the woman, who was bending over her assailant.

"Are you all right?" she asked...

The End

AUTHOR'S NOTE

If you've read Hollow, you'll know this is the point Wendy meets Gwen, the serial killer who just wants to see beauty in the moment of death.

In another life, they could have been friends. Unfortunately, things don't go that way, do they?

Thank you for following Wendy's journey from a troubled child to the 'sweet old lady' we see in Hollow. She also appears in MirrorMirror, speaking to ghost talking Cassidy and his sister, Jazz. If only they knew the truth…!

Do you feel sorry for Wendy? Do you see her loneliness and appreciate the need just to be needed? To be liked? To have friends? Or, is she a cold blooded killer who'll get what she deserves? Please, let me know!

For those who've yet to meet Gwen and her wife Amanda, here's Hollow…

It was just an experiment. Simply kill one person to see the beauty in the moment of death. See if it filled the void within her. It didn't. Not did it the next time. Or the next. Gwen is an ordinary person. Wife to Amanda and mother to Grace and Alexandra. Suddenly, she is no longer ordinary, as she finds herself battling her urges ad demons before she hurts those closest to her.

But, is it already too late?

ABOUT THE AUTHOR

Shaun Allan is a bestselling, award winning author who writes multiple genres, including psychological horror, introspective and emotive poetry, young adult and children's. He has appeared on Sky TV to debate publishing, is a Wattpad Creator and Adim Founding Creator, and been commissioned to write companion stories for such movies as The Purge: Anarchy, Sinister II, The Boy, A Quiet Place, IT and Amazon Prime's Panic series. He also holds regular writing workshops at local schools. Many of his personal experiences are woven into the points of view and senses of humour of his characters, along with the places in and around his home town. His novel Sin has been adapted into a Chapters mobile game titled Straitjacket Lover and was optioned for television.

Shaun lives with his manic dog, Ripley (believe it or not). He works full time and, though his life feels as hyper as his dog, it probably isn't.

You can read more from Shaun at:

www.shaunallan.co.uk

Facebook / Instagram / Threads / TikTok

@singularityspoint

X

@singularityspnt

ALSO BY SHAUN ALLAN
Sin

Hollow

MirrorMirror

Pieces of Me

Dark Places

Darker Places

Dorthy

And the Meek Shall Walk

HERO

Cell